Emz Portraits and Crafts
United Kingdom
Website: www.emzportraitscrafts.wordpress.com
Twitter: @emzportraits

First published in Great Britain by Aloe Jimmy Publishing in 2016
The right for Emma Morrissey to be identified as the author of this work has been asserted by her in accordance with the Copyright, Designs and Patents Act 1988.

ISBN: 978-0-9926276-9-0

British Library Cataloguing-in-publication Data

A catalogue record for this book is available from the British Library

Cover design and inside illustrations by Emma Morrissey BA hons
The publishers' policy is to use paper manufactured from sustainable forests.

Published by Aloejimmy Publishing 2016.

ACKNOWLEDGMENTS

I'd like to thank my Mum, for always supporting me through every up and down, this past 18 months has been very tough for us and at times I've really struggled to keep things together, thank you for helping me create craft stall props, the evening chats when I couldn't sleep, and thank you for always believing in me, I love you Mum!

Thank you to Jimmy and James, the passion to write books is never ending and it's a drive I hope will continue as we keep the magic coming, thanks for your friendship and for getting my books published, I look forward to creating more magic with you.

Thank you to everyone who has helped me get started in the business world, I have learned so much and now see myself in the light of a business woman and am such a strong person for it, thank you David, Jane, Tim, Nicky, Caroline, Frances and everyone else, you know who you are, thanks Macmillan for the chats when we needed them, if I have missed anyone out, please accept my apologies.

Thank you to Mark, for your support in many things.

Last but not least, Thanks Mike, for being my inspiration.

GOTHIC LITERATURE

A collection of Gothic short stories

By Emma Morrissey BA Hons

AUTHORS NOTE

"I would like to thank you sincerely for purchasing this book,

Here you will find it filled with tales of dark stories of several interests and contain many dark and gothic themes, from vampires, stone relics and medieval times,

I hope you enjoy reading it, as much as I have enjoyed writing it"

Emma Morrissey BA Hons 2016

CONTENTS

THE PRINCESS AND THE VAMPIRE

Prelude

Nothing could have prepared me for this part of my life, no
amount of warning, advice or care has ever sunk into the
curious nature which was my naïve mind at the tender age of
twenty, I craved the danger, it made me feel alive, it showed
me things, things I thought only existed in horror stories we
used to read at bedtime around the coal fireplace; it wasn't
until that day, that I was brought up to the surface, out of my
usual delicate state of petticoats, corsets and tea on fathers
porch with my baby Sister and Mother sat sewing the moth
eaten nightclothes, much to my Mothers disgust, as the village
church neighbouring us is being treated for the creatures. To
finally know the truth I knew had been kept from me for so
many years, that day, I lived.

≈

Living in Victorian England, the day slowly drawing to a
close, the house was quiet as usual, deep into the night as it
swallowed any light from the chilled sky, my parents and
baby sister sleeping soundly.

It was true to say that I'd had a privileged and sheltered
upbringing, I was loved, cared for and wanted for nothing,
dressed in the finest clothes as father was a lawyer and would
see to it that we were a perfect reflection of the status he so
eagerly worked to obtain.

1

Alas, this type of life, this kind of existence had its downfalls, for all the love I had, I was lonely, for all the riches, I was unfulfilled, for all the care, I was alone.

The sheltered bubble of privilege has become my shell of pitiful existence and I'd never felt so empty.

Midnight and I can't sleep, the sound of owls and the distant call from the wolves on the hills lured me into dark dreams and had done for the past few evenings; my chest heaving as I'm taken over by the cold chill that floods my room as candlelight disappears; this dream, this dark dream has kept me from sleep again and again as I'm transported to a forest, alone in only my nightgown and black caped coat as my feet sit tight inside the small heels of my black shoes; the icy chill flowing up my long legs as I wrap myself tight in the heavy hooded material, a mist surrounds my ankles as I tread slowly, hearing the crunch and crackle of the dead leaves beneath my soles.

In the distance I'm brought to a large building, a rather breath-taking one, as the mist clears out of its way, I see it's, a castle. Large iron gates stood proud in front of it like a guard, each night I'm brought here and have no recollection of how I got here, or just where exactly I am; all I know is I know the place, my body knows it as I stand in front of it with no hesitation or fear, I know the scent of it, the moisture in the air, the hairs on my neck standing to attention as I know the airs cruel chill that excites and terrifies me.

The wind grows harsh, sweeping my long hair behind my shoulders in its howl as I struggle to keep my balance, looking up at the night sky, I see the jewels of the stars glint back at me; suddenly I feel the wind begin to pick up, twirling and twisting around my legs, propelling me forward atop the iron gates as I peer through the gaps, an old but majestic building of stone stares before me, adorned with thorns and brambles snaking around its walls and towers as they travel upwards, covering mostly all of the castle, the grounds hadn't been attended to for many years it would seem.

Then my eyes stop, fixated on a small flickering light coming from the top window on the right side, the only light, someone must live here? I think to myself, who would possibly live in such a place, in the state it's in?

Suddenly a loud thunderous crack fills my ears, as I lose my balance and cling to the nearby side wall beside the gate to brace myself, as slowly the iron gate begins to move, slowly opening, I begin to feel my heart thump tremendously in my chest as I'm driven forward by my own curiosity.

What are you doing … this is madness, I curse myself, my subconscious trying to take control of this potentially dangerous situation, I don't know why but, every time, this dream, I can't seem to stop myself from walking forward, my curiosity playing the jester as I ignore my initial trepidation and keep walking, occasionally looking back upon the gates which remain open.

My heart is beating so fast now I can barely breathe, gasping for air as I take a few more steps forward, Then without warning, it dawned on me, out of the blue, this dream, reoccurring as often as it does in such fine detail, I don't recall seeing the opposite side of these gates? I've, usually woken up by this point? I begin to ponder, blaming the steak and wine I had for dinner obviously lulling me into an unusually deep sleep, soon, I find myself stood on the steps of the castles entrance, my heart calmed, my legs no longer shaking, my breath easy and slow, the door is grand I must say, adorned with brass and gold detailing around the old door knockers which hold a lion's head with its jaw latched wide open. I don't know … as I reach for the circular handle, gripping it tight in my hand and pull it towards me, it's rather heavy, as I crash it down onto the door as the sound of its pressure rings through my ears, then, a very slight creek pricks my ears up as I see the slowest movement of the door which moves, allowing me just enough space to perch myself between it and the door frame as I squeeze myself inside.

The castle was very grand, even the endless amount of dust and cobwebs couldn't hide its beauty, the detail, the grandeur, it took my breath away.

Then, like a bolt of lightning, I saw a light, coming from the side of me, highlighting the room afar, illuminating an ornate armchair in its patterns as the light danced across the rooms dark walls. Walking closer to it, I stop, shocked still to the stone floor beneath me as I see a shadow move in the light, flowing across the floor as my eyes follow it as I spin around, to see nothing, no one, my heart speeds up as I hear what sounds like, breathing, I blink a couple of times, trying to focus as I realise where I am, staring blankly at the ceiling of my bedroom. The castle now a distant part of my nights digestion, but secretly, desperately awaiting the next chance to drift off into the walls of the castle, curious to find out more about its history and just what lived inside it, until then, I am destined to go about my day, as today's upcoming party function floods my mind as I start to come round from my dream. The covers curled around my feet, my chest heaving, as my nightdress is crumpled into a pool of silk and lace around my hips as I must have tossed and turned in the night.

Such parties always filled me with dread, despite the happy day being the christening of my Baby Sister, these functions were always very large and had the entire cities eyes on it.

The day drags on as I'm forced to sit at the head of the table as my Father makes a short speech, the table is dressed and adorned with many delicacies for all to feast upon; taking a deep breath I feel a pang of guilt, the boredom and false modesty of people always dampens my mood. Placing the napkin across my gown, I notice my hands, draped in lace as my sleeves sit comfortably above my hands, my attention falls to that of my waiter, drawing the wine and placing the meals before us, his hands did not bare such luxury as they appeared rough and scarred, the stress and work of the day mapped them like at atlas of the kitchen he worked from.

Suddenly I am saddened once more, my upbringing meant I never needed to work, although I crave what it feels like to take pride in one's job, to sweat, toil and work for my living, out of all of my female family members, I am the only one who is unfulfilled at this such existence, filled with waiters, butlers and constant tea parties and public engagements, my mind, my body craved more.

"Victoria ... Victoria darling, I have someone I'd like you to meet" said the voice of my Mother, snapping me out of my thoughts as she flows over to me in her lilac ruffled gown, how she managed to call my name so perfectly in that constrictive corset always beguiled me, as I turn and kiss her on the cheek as I spot the man she is referring to over the shoulder of my Mother, a man not much taller than myself walks towards me, in a red velvet jacket and frilled white dress shirt, he is a bundle of nerves as I curtsy slightly to him as he reaches for me with a shaking hand as I extend my own to him which he takes and raises to his lips, his palm sweaty, his lips dry as they brush my soft skin, is this the man my parents have been telling me so much about? I wonder to myself; we have a very brief conversation as he struggles to hold his voice as he stutters and stumbles over his words like a ball tumbling down the stairs, we have nothing in common and unfortunately Seamus was not my idea of a dream man that my parents have been portraying him as, I have to get away, this is unbearably tense.

"It's been very nice to meet you Seamus ... I must..." I begin as my eyes slowly dart to the far corner of the room as the waiters descend to clear the dinner table which is slowly dismantled ready for the celebratory dance, a tradition our family have taken part in for generations to welcome each child into the family. My eyes settle upon a man, stood stock still against the stone white walls of our village hall, seeing my stare, he bows his head slightly forward in acknowledgment, raising his hand to me as he takes a sip from the glass he is clutching, his stare made more evident by his towering form as he stands seemingly unnoticed by the towns people, he posed quite the attraction as my eyes search his appearance, long dark brown hair tied back illuminating his fine chiselled features with a slight smile curling at the corner of his pale pink lips, his broad shoulders wrapped in midnight blue - almost black velvet, escalating down into a long tailored jacket, shadowing tailored trousers and black leather boots, suddenly I noticed an ornate buckle on his belt as it shimmered as the light caught it.

"Excuse me Seamus ..." I say excusing myself as I make my way towards the mysterious man, I am blocked by a small group of people who I quickly brush past, to see the man gone, disappeared as I search around the room for him, my eyes glazing over each person as I make my way to each available space in this large hall, alas, he seems to have completely disappeared from my sight, I haven't seen him before, around the town or, anywhere come to think of it, who was he?

Later that day, back at home, I am consumed by the thoughts of the man I saw at the event in the towns hall, I can't get his image out of my mind, I know I hadn't met him before at any previous grand do and my parents did several throughout the year, it perplexed me that he seemed to go completely unnoticed, almost blending into the surroundings like an ornament; and yet, something about him seemed vaguely familiar, be it his towering stature, the warm glow of his eyes or the amused smile he greeted me with, I need to know who he was.

Soon I am brought back to reality by the sound of my Father calling me, turning around I see him, his usual smiling self as he totters towards me, taking my arm in his as I get the feeling we are about to go on one of our little 'chats', usually consisting of him telling me that I need to find a suitor and get married, this is something he has always reminded me of, my parents had an array of worthy suitors already planned for me to pick from, plenty of money and coming from a good family, 'A match made in heaven' as my Mother would say, however, I have tried to explain my desire to marry for love not for circumstance, much to my parents dismay but at the tender age of twenty, my Father has been trying to pair me up before my twenty first birthday, a sobering thought which makes my heart sink as we walk arm in arm into the patio together, my Father lowering his head slightly, something I have always taken as a sign that he was about to say something which makes him very uncomfortable, his brow furrowing as I take a deep breath.

"Victoria darling … your Mother and I have been very disheartened at your refusal of several worthy young gentlemen who would do you the honour of taking your hand in marriage." My Father begins, his tone snipped as he turns his head towards me, waiting for a reply, for the first time in my life I gave the first honest response;

"Father … I appreciate yours and Mothers time into finding potential husbands however, I have tried to explain before … and I know that you have my best interests at heart and I know how many parties and meetings you have both taken in order to find such men … but … I don't want to be packaged like a prize trophy to a man I don't know … I want to marry for love … I will be certain it will be a man of some wealth and as of the circles I am in, I would only be around men of such … I just wish you would both respect my wishes as I am a women now and can make my own decisions, it makes me feel so very young and useless when such a big part of my life and well … my future is being made for me" I explain, feeling the breath drain from my lungs as I begin to feel rather light headed, afraid of my Fathers reaction, as such honesty is often seen as an insult or disrespect, I await a scolding.

To my surprize, he does not speak, lowering his head and sighing heavily, a look of sadness covers his alabaster skin as strands of his silvering hair begin to dance in the light breeze of the early evening.

"Victoria … you are my eldest Daughter … and the first in line for my fortune when the time comes for me to move from this earth … I … have longed to see this radiant woman stand before me … with her own mind, her own spirit and her honesty …" he begins as I feel my eyes begin to fill with tears at a response which has truly shocked me as I see no anger in his eyes.

"Our main priority is your happiness and although I still stand by our choice of worthy men for you … I cannot force you into an unhappy future … this would only bring upon the one thing I have always feared, and your Mother as well … forcing you into such an important decision would surely alienate you from us and that is something we cannot bare … you are free to choose a man of your taking … on the one condition .. that he be from a good, honest family background and has the riches and circumstances to provide for you … all other details are solely down to you now … my sweet, sweet princess" he says, pulling me into a tight hug, the first I feel I have had as an adult, such an embrace was saved for when I was much younger, playing in the garden grounds with my toys and climbing trees with the servants children.

That evening felt overwhelmed with an unusual and welcomed calmness, it meant a lot to me to have my Fathers blessing on such a life-changing decision for my future and although I had no one in particular in mind, I was so pleased to have that burden lifted, like a ton of bricks removed from my shoulders at long last.

That night I dreamt again, the castle, the grounds, only this time, I made it up the stairs, the steps uneven and covered in dust, the banister leaving small imprints of my fingertips as I cling to it as it begins to spiral around following the twisting staircase.

On the second floor I find a narrow hallway in front of me, dimly lit with candelabras, highlighting the rouge wallpaper and cream feature walls, decorated with gold ornaments, jewels of the finest emerald and rubies on the nearby light fittings, all glistening back at me as I walk gingerly down the hall, following a light, the one from outside in the top window that took my attention from the castles gates. Drawing closer to the room, I hear a dull, distant humming, pleasant and not intimidating as my feet continue where my heart has stopped, my heart coming up into my mouth as fear comes over me at just what the hell I am doing.; suddenly I am knocked of all sense as I perch myself behind the door, looking into the room.

"I would guess by now that you know this is not a dream … I knew you'd come ... at last … my sweet, darling Victoria!" said a voice, deep, smooth and somewhat familiar as I stop short of the door, the light shining from behind it, plunging my current place of standing into complete darkness.

"Who are you … how do you know my name?" I ask, feeling my legs shake to match my trembling voice.

"You do not remember me … but … your body does … you are curious and I had waited … waited so long for you … in your unconscious state of dreaming, you were brought here … back to me … where you belong, where you are safe … where you are … mine!" he continued as I open the door a little further … to reveal a grand chair, tall, gold and red cushioned, perched near a fireplace which crackled and flickered with glowing embers; there he was, stood with his back to me, one hand on the corner of the chair, looking upon the fire as the flames danced.

His tall frame painted the perfect silhouette, midnight blue-almost black velvet jacket, long dark hair tied back into a long ponytail, the man from the celebration ball in the town hall?

Suddenly he turns, slowly as I drink him in, his expression soft, his posture straight and regale in its appeal as he bows his head gracefully with a smile.

"I am Lord Vancampt ... I .... am your husband" he exclaims, shifting his gaze to the window for a split second, unable to look at my shocked expression.

"My husband ... no ... this is ... I'm not ... I've never been with a man, I'm not married ... who are you, what do you want with me?" I say, my voice slightly raised though shaking as he stands still, one arm braced behind his back as a pained look covers his face.

"You can't deny it Victoria ... you do know me ... it's your spirit that recognises these chambers, bringing you here in your dreams, these were not merely figments of your imagination Victoria, they are your memories ... now you are here ... in the flesh, real, if you did not know this place, then please tell me ... why did you return ... why do you long to have these, so called dreams, to bring you back here ... seeking this ... seeking me ... that's why I showed myself to you in the hall, to see whether you would seek me once more?" he continued, slowly moving past the chair, walking slowly towards me, his tall frame overshadowing mine as he comes closer, I do not move, I can't but ... to look at him, something does seem vaguely, slightly familiar but I am at a loss as I start to feel light headed.

Suddenly he reaches for me, his cold hand clasping to my upper arm as I gasp at the cool sensation.

"Breathe Victoria ... you always were prone to such things ... just breathe ... I won't hurt you" he says, helping me over to the chair which I have admired since I came into this room, the soft, smooth velvet cushions taking my weight perfectly as I sit down, seeing him perch himself on the edge of the nearby table, looking at me with concern as he hands me a glass of water.

Sipping slowly, I start to feel myself return, I cannot fathom just where I am, apart from the fact that somehow ... I do recall ... something ... why have I kept returning here, what possessed me to seek it out ... I silently ask myself as I feel myself begin to shake.

"You crave something more ... I can sense it ... I can hear you at night in your restless slumber ... your chest heaving, your breath hitching as you try, clinging to each sight of my castle that fills your eyes ... you come back, every night ... without calling or summon and you have been here before ... many years ago; your dreams filled with the memories of our time here ... together" he begins, as I feel, curiosly, my shaking subside.

"You were taken from me ... many moons ago, in a sickness rarely felt by creatures such as us ... in that moment, you promised me you would return to me, I held you close and since that night, I waited patiently for you ... through the endless births of your ancestors ... waiting ... praying that one day, your spirit would take hold once more ... in a new form and bring you back to me ... I have watched you grow into the most beautiful, curious, generous creature that I remember you to be … born into a loving family, perfect to shape my gorgeous princess … oh how I have missed you so!" he exclaimed, his voice breaking as I see a tear roll down his pale cheek as he reached his fingers towards my face, this time, I did not flinch, fixated on the blue orbs of his eyes, sorrowful and pained as his fingers grazed ever so lightly across my face, caressing my cheek as I closed my eyes at the sensation, I knew that touch, a calmness flooded me.

"You crave to know life … you have been so sheltered… but I am so glad of it … for it has given your spirit time to grow into this … strong minded women I always remembered you to be … you long for more, you have been so … starved …of what true love you longed for … love that you have written about in your diaries over this past decade … you are so … innocent, just as you were the night I first met you … lost in the grounds of my castle, running away from an argument that frightened you, and yet you step foot into my castle, finding comfort in me … oh my love … I have longed for this moment „,when my love would return … but … you look … different, your hair a darker shade then I recall, your skin not the porcelain I remember and your body frame shorter, but … your spirit blazes just the same, it knows me, doesn't it my love … when I get .. this … close … to you? …" he whispered, I could feel his breath on my cheek as he stepped closer to me, taking my hand in his, feeling the soft, cool skin against my own as I looked up at him through teary eyes.

"Your hands look different yet your touch … feels just the same soft caress it always was, your scent the same … I wouldn't change a thing … accept that which you wish for … your spirit longs to be with me … where you are safe, loved and belong, together, in this, our castle, our home, I can make you … the woman you long to be … if you will have me … my Victoria … my life … my love … my wife …" he continued, his mouth inches from mine as he lent down slightly, my chest heaving as I cannot speak, brushing his face over my hand like a cat as he got down on one knee, reaching behind him to produce a small black box.

"But you must undertake a sacrifice, of your human form once more, as you did those many centuries ago, for you see … we were both … and I remain … immortal" he continued, opening the box before me to reveal a ring, a bright sparkling ice white jewel surrounded by gold banding, woven in a filigree design forming the letter 'V', staring back at me as I felt myself begin to weep, never before had I been given such a choice, a choice for a life that felt right, I felt no fear, no doubt, as minute by minute, memories flooded my mind.

"This was your wedding ring … that I presented to you on that night you became mine … I have kept it, waiting for the day where I could present it to you once more … but I must confess, I am very uncertain as to your response, I recall that night … here, in this room, your first words back to me and I long to hear them again … but I know … it is a very unlikely circumstance for you to utter the same … but I do hope, like the smitten man you have tamed me to be" he continued, his face stained with glistening tears, made more by the flames that picked up on their watery trails.

"… You are my life … my love … my knight … Victor Vancampt … yes!" I said, followed by a moment of complete confusion as to just where those words came from … he didn't say his first name so how could I know? Suddenly I smile, closing my eyes, suddenly my mind filled with yet more images of our lives together, and in particular, our wedding day and the night he proposed to me on bended knee.

"Oh … my darling, sweet, princess … what such a tremendous women you are, you recall your words to me, how I love you so, my Victoria …" he said, placing the ring on my finger as it slips on without struggle, as I feel its weight on my finger as the gem shines up at me.

With that he smiles, wiping the remaining tears away from his cheeks, standing up before me, I feel his hands placed either sides of my cheeks as I close my eyes, my heart pounding, opening my eyes to see Victor smiling softly, shaking his head slightly, almost in disbelief as he muttered "I love you …" pressing his lips against mine in a soft, gentle kiss.

We spent several hours talking about our time in this castle, the good and the bad, times when the castle had been subject to the mighty flood and Victor used his power to keep the slowly rising water away from my bed chambers, fearful that it would ruin the precious silks and satins he had bought me; and the night of our wedding, where several of his family joined us as we took a boat journey around the castles moat, several candles lighting each end of the boat, it was said that doing this journey three times around the outside of your domain would protect our lives together by sealing our love, Victor went on to tell me how this did not work, as I was taken from him, unknown to us, there was a slight break in the journey around the moat, hence love had a hole, this is where my sickness entered.

He took me around the tour of the castle as I recalled my favourite places to settle, the grand library where I would read books when I couldn't sleep, the kitchen where Victor bought me drinks to settle my nerves on a stormy night, our bedroom, where we first sealed our love.

"What about my family though, surely they will be worried as to where I am?" I asked, as a pang of worry came over me like a freak wave.

"Your spirit is a very strong one my love ... a spell was cast on your family the night you were born ... that once you had returned to your true life, your family would go into an almost trance like state, in this state, they are not concerned for you, nor grieve for you, they simply know you are safe and happy, I can assure you they feel no pain, they are fine" he explained, before too long we sat in the study with goblets of wine as he made me some dinner, fresh fish from the moat he told me, this time of year, several fish would shelter themselves in or moat away from the icy waters, along with mint potatoes, grown from our grounds outside, it was mouth-watering; a much welcome sensation as I felt like I had not eaten for days, after finishing the last mouthful, Victor got on his knees in front of my chair with a look of dismay on his face as he began to explain what the immortal transformation would be like.

"It will feel to you ... like a sickness when the venom seeps into your blood, you will be very ill, but only for a short time, a few minutes ... you will be reborn to me, as your true former self ... be brave my love ... I will be by your side, I will not leave you ... it does relent, I promise you" he whispered, with a reassuring stroke of his hand across my cheek.

With that, I see a look of hunger cloud his eyes, leaving an unsteady yet aroused feeling to sweep through me as I feel his teeth lightly graze against my neck, leaving soft, wet kisses as my eyelids flutter closed, followed by a sharp excruciating pain that takes my breath away as I scream, feeling his hold become tighter as a hot white pain floods my skin as it burns, holding me at arm's length for a moment he looks down upon me, his lips painted with the ruby droplets of my blood, my eyes become hazed as I writhe in knotted agony … like a thousand red hot needles piercing my skin, after several minutes of shuddering and shaking, soon the pain begins to subside, I remain in his arms as he brings me forward to rest my head in the crock of his shoulder as he hushes me softly, stroking my hair lovingly;

"Shhhh my love … I'm so sorry my sweet … I can never get used to seeing you in such pain at my hand … shhhh it's almost over my love … shhhh" he whispers; for a while I don't know if I'm even alive … once my eyes come into focus they set upon my love … as he smiles at me and places a kiss on my forehead, he brings a mirror towards me, looking at my reflection … I see me … but a more radiant version staring back at me, I have purer, porcelain skin, my hair … perfect, not a split end in sight, my eyes sparkle a deep hue of green and blue and I look ... happy.

"I have a reflection?" I ask, looking over at Victor with a confused look over my face as he smiles in amusement.

"Yes my love … you are not fully immortal yet … the full process will take several days, after that, your reflection will disappear, but you will be able to see your image in your mind's eye … so do not fret, you will be able to get your makeup on without a mirror" he jested.

"What about my clothes …" I begin as Victor cuts me off, raising his hand in a motion that indicates he has thought of everything.

"We have servants my love … they will help you with your corsets and anything else you require, but as I said, your mind's eye will be very powerful, so you will be able to do them yourself if you wanted to … do not worry … it will become normal again to you in time" he says, his voice laced with reassurance as I try to calm my worried mind.

I become slightly perplexed as I place my hand over my chest, looking back up to see Victor who had a soft amused smile on his face:

"My heart is still beating?" I say softly, hearing my voice, I almost don't recognise it, it sounds, smoother, softer, I feel so, confused but there is not a hint of any such confusion to be heard in my voice.

"I know, it's a strange sensation I would imagine when you are not expecting it … don't be fooled, you are immortal, partially, but I recalled the very first time you underwent this, the first thing you said to me, wasn't that you felt the cold chill of your skin, or that you craved blood, but that you missed the feel of your heartbeat, so I thought it would be good for you to have that same sensation a little while longer; as you may recall, I do have some supernatural power, so … I cast a spell when I began the process of changing you, it will give you the feeling of a heartbeat, but you should notice, it is much faster, it will last as long as you need it, until you are comfortable in your new form" he explained, placing his hand on mine as it rested upon my chest.

It was here I stayed, my old life slowly coming back to me as the days went on, Victor was at my side often, tending to me as I underwent the full transformation, each night I lay in our large bed, wrapped in Victors arms as he stroked my back as I struggled to get accustomed to the sensation of sharing a bed with someone again, but I welcomed the feeling of warmth against me, yet another spell he cast to help me settle, changing his chilled skin to that of a mortals warm temperature. His touch was comforting, his lips loving and I felt nothing but purity from his every move as he made it clear that I was in his every thought.

The servants were kind and after a while, I began to build friendships with them, one in particular, Molly, the youngest of the servant woman, probably not much older than myself, I suspected early twenties; yet I was unsure if they were too, immortal like myself and Victor, but either way it didn't matter, Molly and I spent one night playing hide and seek in the grand castle, finding many places I had yet to discover as I tucked myself in behind stone columns and under grand dining tables, we spent several hours giggling and enjoying each other's girly spirits, it was, fun.

Soon I heard the low chuckle of a voice that brought us to a sudden stop as I turned to see Victor come out of the darkness, a serious expression on his face soon to be replaced by one of amusement as me and Molly both sighed in relief that he wasn't angry.

"Having fun my love?" he inquired, putting his hands behind his back in the gentlemanly fashion that made his long velvet robe curl around him even better.

We just nodded in response as Molly bowed slightly at him and made her way back to her chambers, saying goodnight to me as she left.

"So … you were so bored with our life in our large sleeping quarters that you thought it a good idea to roam the castle in the dead of night with our servant girl?" he asked, a cool, crisp tone to his voice that made me nervous as I opened my mouth to speak, only to find I had no voice to use, my throat closing up in fear as that serious look came over his face once more.

"I … didn't mean …." I began as suddenly Victor rushed up to me and I instinctively moved back, my feet gliding across the cool flooring of the ballroom that the hide and seek game had brought me into.

"So … you want some more … Excitement is that it … you're … unfulfilled with just me in my gentlemanly form … is that it my love?" he asked, his voice now dripping with promises of dark thoughts that made me blush.

"Well … if that's the case … if you're sure … "he began, a smile curling up the edges of his now red lips, when suddenly he pounced, as he began to chase me around the ballroom, giggling I ran, hopelessly, as I felt him reach for me as I swooped out of his reach, curving to throw him off as to my delight he slowed down as I turned to see he had vanished, spinning around on the spot he had gone as I frowned in misunderstanding.

Then, turning in the direction of the door there he stood, several feet away from me, but he looked, different, the robe gone as he stood in entirely black attire, leather? His hair down, surrounding his shoulders, his eyes darker with a seductive smile painted across his lips as he took one step forwards, I blinked to find him directly in front of me, faces inches apart as I took a breath in shock as he reached for me, placing one hand on my cheek, softly caressing it, whilst the other snaked around my waist.

"Excitement hmmm? ... Come here my princess" he whispered, picking me up in his arms like I weighed nothing as he strode out of the ballroom with me laid across his arms.

The next morning I woke up with a smile on my face, my head resting on Victors chest, our arms wrapped around each other, this is where I belong I thought, all the years memories of past times now completely clear, days went on, months, years and I couldn't be happier, Molly and I grew to be best friends and Victor and I became completely and hopelessly in love with each other, this was my home, my life.

"Morning Princess ... are you ok?" the sound of Victors voice knocking me out of my daydream as I turn my head to see him smiling down at me as I cuddle into his chest more, nodding in response.

This was my lot, and what a perfect lot it was, the Princess and her Vampire.

GARGOYLES

Atop a tall, dark tower, stood its sworn protectors, four stone gargoyles, eroded by the years of cold, icy winters that threatened their personalities as all soon became a carbon reflection of one another.

Each night, on the clocks chime of midnight, each one came to life, raising their heavy heads at the moons glow and climbed down from the tower, the pack were in search of the truth of their existence, one which had led to much ruin and dismay. In the hope that they would find what legend had said, they were in search of the stone maiden, their keeper and holder of all earths' secrets behind such relics of old.

The tower, standing above the surrounding twisting trees, had played host to many prisoners in medieval England, gargoyles were said to be the guards of their souls when they passed on, seeing them safely off on their journey to the moons sky, but, the four gargoyles had grown weary of such gloom, this protective ancestry they had been carved into, as each century one is replaced, their destiny of soul guardians had grown tiresome.

Despite the erosion of the gargoyles sharp features, they still maintained a certain charm, the forth of the pack, and the last to be replaced, held the medallion of arms across its chest, a symbol that was said to be given out by the stone maiden to her most worthy leaders.

The forth lead the pack into the forest, past the hooting owls and beyond the creatures that ruled the grounds beneath their tower. Gargoyles moved slowly by nature, walking in fluid, slow motion as their stout stone legs crumpled the fallen leaves as they were flattened into the sole with their heavy feet.

Each gargoyle moved in reflection of the moonlight, powering them as they made their way through the forest, the trees that had grown so tall, casting shadows like a puppet show, momentarily blocking the moons shine, causing the gargoyles to come to a sudden halt, until the branches gave way and the stony creatures could move again, such mystical timing made for much of the forest to be unsearched as their delayed, slow journeys often took them into the early hours with not much ground covered in their travels, the first chirp of a morning bird was their signal to get back to their tower.

"You there ... plain ... what has rain-daze done to you poor stone?" said the maiden, her voice high-pitched and dreamy; "I am sorry for my position lack, I know you have been in search, but many creatures less honest than yourselves search to kill me so I must retain mystery as to keep my whereabouts a secret from such fate ... you crave truth don't you gargoyles?" she asked, her stance still in her stony appearance, as the moon shines down through the leaves, allowing her to move one leg slightly before the other a she walks statically to bend before one of them.

"You are all true watchers of the tower and you have done so very well ... but alas, you are all spiritually sworn to an ancient charm, where you are each keeper of a family tree. The legend tells me of Four gargoyles, that protect four families, in four destinations of the earth, Iceland, China, Mexico and Russia ... sometime soon, when I feel the earths turn slow, this will be your time, your time to go back to your spiritual homes and protect those families ... you will know when the time is right ... now be gone, back to the tower, the sun is beginning to rise" she said as the gargoyles began to turn their heavy heads, looking in the direction of the tower.

Each one moving their stony legs as far as the moon would allow them between gaps in the trees for the moon to shine upon them, giving them the power of movement. Staring up at their perches, they climbed the tower, one foot at a time until they were settled once more, back to the cries of the prisoners, the sounds of fights breaking out beneath them, knowing they had more souls, soon in need of being carried to the skies, waiting, for the day their true destiny would be upon them and they would be transported back to their four families, where they belonged.

Gargoyles

26

THE TITANIUM SWORD

In a small clearing in Southern England, there stood an old cottage near a train track. In the basement laid a sword, made of the strongest titanium, said to have slayed the Romans and had been handed down through the Tudor period in Great Britain. It is said that it holds great power to whomever holds it, giving the bearer the power of ten strong warriors, encrusted with emeralds from Egypt in its handle, its power is thought to be from the ancient Egyptians, stories told in each family of a great fight between the pharaohs of old; to which the father of the youngest pharaoh King, placed an ancient spell on the sword, to ensure his only Son could not be slayed, it is said that it is this power which lay in the swords handle.

One day on a cool crisp spring morning, a young boy of a poor family was collecting firewood with his Father, his Mother in the kitchen baking for the family, after his chores the young boy would play in the yard, dreaming of great battles played by him and the neighbour boys. Wearing his Mothers bed sheets as capes and a crown fashioned from the kitchen fruit bowl, the boy played like it had been forged from the finest jewels and his cape flowing like the richest velvet as they fought with sticks for swords.

Over the years the boy had grown into a fine young man, seeing many tragedies in his young life, the sickness of his Baby Sister, the flood that threatened his Fathers crops, the birth of his little Brother as his Mother laid in sickness for six months of the pregnancy; on the boys seventh birthday, the skies grew blood red, as his Father displayed a look of horror as he rushed outside onto the porch with a rifle in his hand, "Trouble in coming, look after your Mother" he whispered.

His Father was gone for several weeks, up in the Town's main dwelling, the boy could hear the cries and calls of several people in distress, everyday tending to his Mother and praying for his Fathers safe return. One day, the Father came back, his hair wild, his face sporting cuts and wounds over his body, his Son took him into the kitchen to tend to him, hiding his dishevelled and bloody appearance from his Mother.

Every week he would go into the woods with his Father to hunt for food, learning to use weapons his Father had hoped he would also use to defend them when trouble came to the town.

On the eve of the boys eightieth birthday, he had become the successor to his Father who had grown weary from the houses upkeep, leaving his Son to fend for the families wealth and wellbeing. Earlier that decade there was an outcry by the locals who were fighting against the higher classes, who sent a declaration to the authorities to order poorer folk out of the town, for fear they may tarnish the reputation of the flourishing City by their lack of wealth and position; the boy's Father lead a group to the high Council, to fight for their rights to stay in the town they had grafted for, for so many years.

"In these times you wish to order us out of our homes, when you sit comfortably in your big houses and kept land, houses built by us, land kept by us, it is us who have allowed you to sit so comfortably, without us you have nothing, we will not be removed!" the Father cried, with the locals men to back him, the high classes backed down, only to be reawakened eight years later; the family had suffered much in that time, flood, disease and the Father had grown weak, it was his Son who had the families wellbeing at the fore front of his mind now, to follow in his Father's footsteps.

Now older and struggling, the Father left this to his Son, in the hope he would restore some peace where he had failed.

The town's once quite ambience had become a distant memory, the shouts of many carried on the wind, reminding the Father of past times rather forgotten, and trouble was coming. All of the discord in the villages got the unwanted attention of the neighbouring City, riddled with crime and violence, one warm afternoon, a group from the rival City came into town, carrying weapons looking sure to find trouble.

After dinner, the Father took his Son to one side for an important talk, looking upon his Son, his face weathered and covered in sweat,

"You must go my Son, defend your Country's honour and protect our family, what I am about to tell you must remain a secret, you must tell no-one do you hear me?" he said, his expression speaking of a serious time that worried the young man who looked upon his Father in concern.

"Go into the basement and look for the latch to the trapdoor in the corner of the floor, lift it up and you will find a sword … the sword has been in our family for generations after your Great, Great Grandfather won it in a bloody battle fighting for his King and Country … you must use it … it is said to be very powerful and obtains a magic that is very rare and dangerous in the wrong hands … no man to hold it has ever been defeated or injured in battle, use it my Son, to keep your family and town safe from these barbarians!" the Father said, placing his hand on his Sons in a silent prayer. "Make me proud" he whispered.

The young man made his way into the basement and uncovered the sword, taking the advice of his Father, he said goodbye to his Parents and Siblings, turning to see the sky cover his gaze in blood red as it had done many years before, taking a deep breath, he made his way into the centre of the town, each step of his slightly down trodden shoes reminding him of what he was about to do, taking a deep breath he braced himself, ready for battle with his sword in hand as he stopped upon the hill overlooking the towns high Council buildings and small shops. Windows were broken, furniture and part of buildings now laid battered on the dusty ground, any previous memory of lush grass beds now a muddy mixture of wheel tracks and footsteps of the rival people, suddenly something took his eye, as he stared upon it trying to focus; he saw three guys, vests torn, bare feet, looking to be the trouble makers, as they made a move to a nearby building, breaking down the door of a house, a scream filled his ears as one of the guys ran inside and pulled out a young girl from behind the door, who struggled against him as the other guys just laughed, patting her head as she tried to fight him off, kicking her legs out towards them.

The young man felt his grip on the sword get stronger as he knew what he had to do, feeling rage travel through him, he ran down the hill, his feet going faster than he could control as soil broke up beneath his feet, he yelled after the guys who turned in surprize, seeing the sword and looking amongst each other.

"Stay back boy … you have no power here, you are no match for us, we are nearing the takeover of this place …" the first guy explained, holding the girl to him as she tried to stop her screams through fear of being hurt; looking at the sword, the man smiled and scoffed at it.

"And I'm pretty sure one sword isn't going to be enough to take on all of us … go back to Daddy, before you get really hurt!" he said, laughing, as he and the other guys taunted him.

"Boy? I am many things guys, but a Boy is certainly not one of them, I as just as strong as you, if not more … If you are as … strong as you claim … prove it, let her go and fight me … go on!! If you have the guts … guys like you are nothing, with your arrogant walks and preying on the weak and defenceless … only because you don't have the courage of your convictions to take on someone as strong, or stronger than you … come on then big Boy … fight me!" he said, wielding his sword ready for a blow, the guy let the girl go, throwing her to one side as she crashed into the nearby window, yelling in pain as blood ran down her arm where it cut her slightly, she stood up quickly, holding her arm and ran away, calling for her parents.

Turning around, the guy picked up a long piece of metal, covered in oil and looked to have been burnt, throwing it back behind himself, he took a swing at the young man, yelling as he did, holding the sword up to meet it, the long piece of metal shattered into thousands of small pieces, following a bright flash of light as it did so, the force of the crash bringing the swords tip to hit the ground as the soil began to form a large crack; the bully fell back to the ground by the force of it, his chest heaving as he got to his feet and looked to his friends who all backed off, making their way away from the him, who followed them quickly, looking back at the sword as they ran.

Looking up at the sky the boy felt a harsh wind, carried on it, the sounds of more battles, taking a deep breath, he followed the sound which led him into the City further, soon he was met by a horrendous scene, soon to catch the attention of some of the towns men who flocked before him, spying the sword he carried, clutched tight in his hand, soon a group of over a hundred men stood before him, ready to go into battle with him as their leader, the boy's father was right, it must have had great power for these men to have such a sudden change of heart and back him.

Holding their make-shift weapons above their heads they followed the young man into the onslaught, to battle the rival towns men, there were many hours of fighting as the people grew weary, the young man made his way through each obstacle, no fear in his eye as the sword slayed each of the rivals, to ensure calm to his town.

The coming days felt different, calmer, the cries of people stopped, the sound of crashing and clinking of make shift weapons now ceased, the sky now glowed blue, with clouds passing by his gaze as he looked up and smiled, looking down at his hand, the sword glowing from the sun as it caught the light of the emeralds glowing back at him.

"Thanks Dad" he whispered, gripping it tightly, as he made his way back to his home.

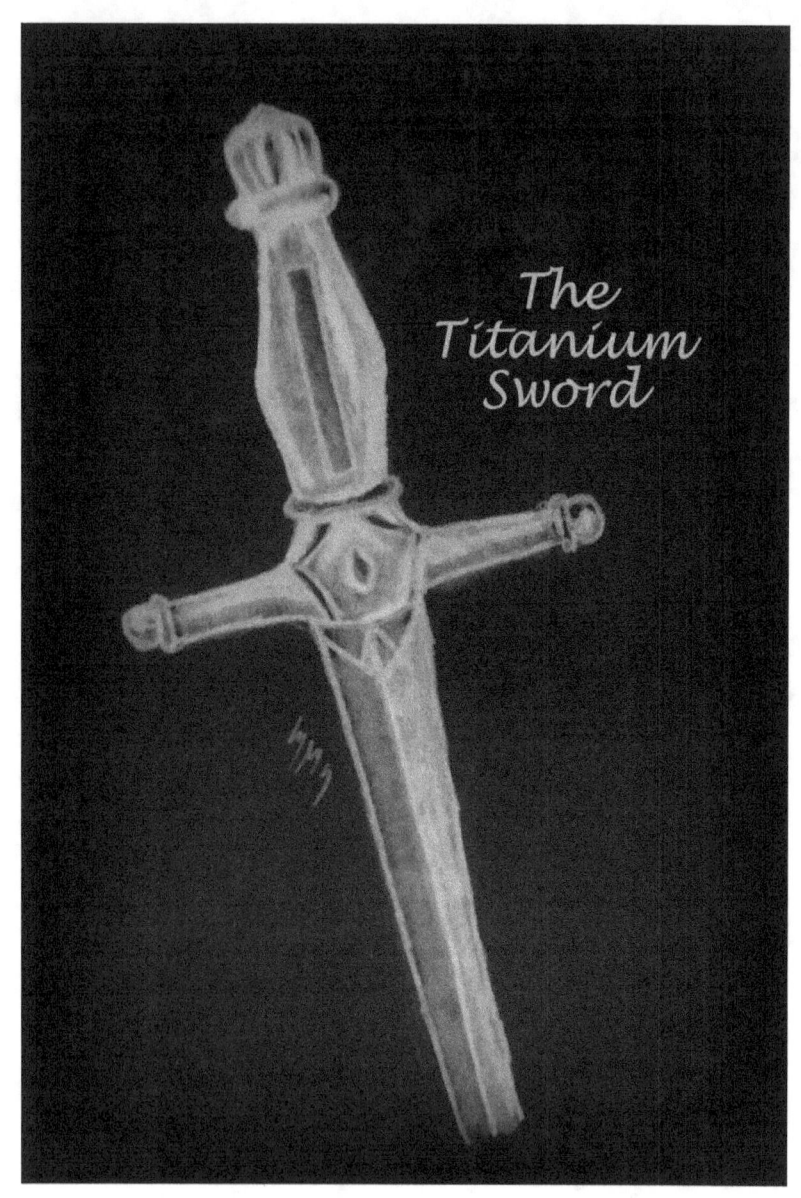

The
Titanium
Sword

BARBARIANS

In medieval Europe there were many people, discord had called for a split, dividing the people into groups, the Wealthy, the Servants, the Warriors and the Barbarians. All of which were sworn to live in harmony at the request of Frances King. These separations had caused much hurt between families whom kept friendships from opposing groups, too much criticism and in some cases war had plagued the streets for months.

The Kings daughter remained innocent and pure of heart despite the history of the lands discord. In a night of violence with the darkness of the night sky, with nothing but the moon as their lighting, the young woman hid in her chambers as she heard fighting commence in the downstairs hallway below; hiding beneath her bed ensuring the blankets had an overhang to disguise most of the gap so that she could not be seen.

≈

Suddenly, I heard footsteps, followed by the crash of my bedroom door being kicked down, I placed my hand over my mouth to silence any sound as I felt my heart jump into my throat; I saw several pairs of sandaled feet as several men entered, emptying wardrobes, throwing over tables and stealing jewels and gold from my dresser. They seemed to be in some sort of armour, though the position under the bed made for anything above the knee had to be imagined as it was hidden from my view. As the men left I let out a sigh of relief, unable to hold it in any longer, to which the last man turned on his heel, hearing my voice and slowly entered the room once more, edging closer to the bed, I began to shake as his feet inched closer to my bed, suddenly he reached underneath and pulled me out with a strong tug of his bare arm, I screamed and began to cry, bashing my fists against his muscular chest as he covered my mouth with his large hand as I struggled against him.

His armour laid across his bare skin, covered with sweat, tuning me around to face him I recoiled, escaping his grip to raise my arm over my face to protect myself from a suspected attack. Looking into my eyes he raised his finger to his lips and indicated for me to remain silent, with that he pulled me over his shoulder and hid me in the nearby wardrobe as I heard him exit the room with strong heavy footsteps; I sat shaking behind the wardrobe door as my mind began to calm, puzzled by what had just happened, my breathing ragged, my heart thumping, I could hear male voices which slowly became less in volume, did they leave?

He returned, opening the door with a strong fling of his arm, I looked up at him from my knelt position on some boxes, my tear stained face pleading with him, his long dark brown hair matted, his beard travelling down his chin, his skin tanned as his chest heaved before me, beads of sweat running from his temples down onto his chest.

"Please don't hurt me" I sobbed, my voice just above a whisper, his eyes brightened, turning his head to one side, a serious look in his eye,

"I will not hurt you Princess, but I must conceal you, to maintain your safety or you will be killed by my fellow barbarians" he said, his voice deep and serious.

I sat still, my shaking subsided as I frowned in confusion, "Why did you spare me?" I asked, rising to my feet to look him in the eye.

"I've never seen such …." He began, lowering his head, " … pure beauty and I find it most desirable, you are under my protection … all of us are trained to destroy anything that crossed our path … you did not cross mine, I crossed yours and your face … so young, so pure … I don't have the heart to kill you" he said.

Suddenly I began to shake in fear once more, "But … what plan do you have for me … where is my Father?" I asked, looking around as the worst thoughts fill my head.

"Do not ask me that Princess, I have not seen anyone else alive in this palace, I have no plan for you … I … despite my form and nature … am not like my fellow brothers and cousins … I can be brutal, but in a protective manner, I do not know of the ways of a gentlemen nor the ways to behave in company such as yours … but I do know how to hunt for food to keep you alive, to keep you warm and to hide you from a worse fate at the hands of my cousins who would take much more from you than just your riches" he continued, his face stern, he was very tall against my small, meek frame, his arms and chest covered in symbols etched in permanent ink, his lower half covered in armoured skirts of iron and gold, he cast quite the image of a man.

"I think … dare I say … I think that perhaps I am smitten by your purity … I cannot slay something … someone so … angelic" he said.

Awhile after I began to feel rather weak, it had been well over twenty-four hours since the fight began in my home and all the food had either been stolen or eaten, the lack of food was beginning to set in, upon seeing me become so weak before his eyes, he left me to go hunting, coming back an hour later with some meat.

"So what was life like for you growing up?" I asked, helping myself to the meat before me as he carved some, his hunting skills were impressive though I couldn't bear the thought of it, and if it wasn't for being so hungry I might've refused.

"Well it was hard, we had to learn to fend for ourselves, we were taught to fight and not to stop if someone got in our way" he explained as he took a hold of a piece of meat and began to hack into it with an eagerness I had only seen in animals, barely leaving time to breathe between each mouthful as I sat shocked at his animalistic manners, he looked up at me over the now bare bone as he dropped it onto the plate.

"You'll have to forgive me Princess, I do not have gentlemanly manners, I enjoy my food, growing up with my brothers and cousins you had to fight for food or you would starve, such an experience made for our vigour when we so much as smell food; many of my brothers wasted away because they simply weren't quick enough ..." he said, taking a napkin and covering the remains of bone on the plate from my shocked gaze as he continued.

"Our elder who taught us, did not see that there was enough food for us all, he believed those who were worthy would fight to the end, be it for food or power, it was our way to prove to him we were worthy of the title barbarian" he explained, wiping his mouth with the back of his hand as I looked down at my plate, seeing my knife and fork in hand and continued eating.

A thought popped into my head suddenly, thinking of him growing up around hundreds of men.

"So what would happen if you wanted to settle down, get married?" I asked curiously as he laughed, throwing his head back in amusement.

"Hahaha ... no one in this pack has ever broken away so I cannot say, its unheard of, I would guess that we would be disgraced and removed from the pack as quickly as possible, dishonoured" he said.

"Have you ever been with a woman?" I ask, cursing my lips for forming such a personal question to which he smiled, lowering his head as the smile quickly faded.

"Yes I have …but in many ways I haven't, at the dare of my cousins, we were frequent to visits of women in the night who were happy to ease the testosterone in our blood by spending many an hour with us, not a lady such as yourself, I've never been with a lady before" he concluded, as I saw a slight hint of pink cover his cheeks.

"I feel my cheeks begin to burn as I too blush, he called me a lady, giggling internally like a schoolgirl.

"You say you have no manners of a gentleman, yet you speak very well" I say, finishing the last remnants of food as he gulps down his drink, putting the cup down loudly, not realising his strength as I jump.

"Well I suppose I've always wanted to be more than the barbarian I was raised to be, in a time where discord opened opportunity for a challenge in authority, we have been the militaries worst nightmare … causing chaos, we fight with the same vigour and power as them, but without the shields, swords or horseback … I … aside from times when I had no choice but to follow my brothers work … I craved to see the world, meet people of a different class and … come out of this … I am an alpha male Princess, that is true of me and will not change, but I am a gentle giant at heart, I am a protector, not the destroyer I am built to be" he said, his eyes blazing with truth as my heart went to him.

I smile to myself, realising a simple, yet important fact, as I open my mouth to speak,

"I've just realised, I don't know your name?" I ask awaiting a response to see his expression change once more, he looked disturbed.

"We weren't given names, our elder thought it too familiar, we are known by letters or numbers, they call me R" he said, rubbing his hands nervously up his legs as he looked increasingly uncomfortable, the sight of him perched on such a small stall was an amusing sight to me I have to admit.

"Ok well that changes now … how about … Raven?" I say, removing the napkin from my lap and placing it on the table as I move to stand, he smiles and nods his head, his lips parting for a second.

"What is your name Princess?" he asks, reaching his hand for mine as I look upon it nervously.

"My name is Caroline … Princess Caroline" I reply, placing my hand in his as his large, long fingers curl around my small hand, suddenly I am brought back down to earth by a thud, literally, a thud, Raven turns to me with a startled look in his eye,

"We must leave, now, my brothers must have returned in search of me, I must hide you!" with that he grabs me and hoists me up over his shoulder.

"Where are we going?" I ask, feeling my head bob along as he stomps through the houses hallways, he doesn't answer me, as I feel him stopping every so often for fear of being caught by the other barbarians. Soon we are outside as he puts me back to my feet as we stand close to the houses brickwork, Raven looking around the corner, seeing that the coast is clear for us to make our getaway.

"I don't quite know what this plan involved but your brothers are right there!" I whispered, seeing Raven glare back at me in annoyance as his brothers came in our direction. With one swift motion he grabbed my arm and I was lifted off of my feet onto his back as he began climbing the side of the building, perching his heels in the bricks spaces as he went until we reached my balcony, climbing over the top as we sat silently behind the few small bushes that hide my bedroom from onlookers eyes.
Soon we heard the voices grow distant as we both let out a sigh.

"I knew it wouldn't be safe to go ahead of them, they were more likely to catch up with our whereabouts eventually, they are here for me; barbarians such as us are taught often, not to retrace our steps by revisiting the sights of our attacks, as this can bring upon feelings of guilt or remorse which is against our upbringing, so I thought it safer for us to let them go ahead, we will leave in the morning, they would have hit the next town by then, giving us a good, clear trail to find somewhere new, it is not safe for you to remain here Princess" he explained, sweat dripping from his muscles as his armour clung to them like a lifeline.

We sat, nestled amongst the shrubbery which encased my balcony, hidden away from any possible view that would threaten us. That night I slept soundly, to my surprize at awakening with a feeling of refreshment and well rest; I spotted Raven stood near my window, the thin curtains almost see through as the sun shun on them, highlighting Ravens toned figure, he was a vision, I thought, never before had I slept so soundly whilst in the midst of something so chaotic in my life, my Father, being King, had often encouraged many whom were, upset with his seemingly selfish decisions to threaten his rule, this caused for many fights and unrest in the royal household, all of which I was witness to from a very early age, often confined to my bedroom quarters like some sort of prisoner, I could hear the chaos, but was so shut off from everyday life that I had become afraid of it, it was unknown to me, talking to people outside of the royal grounds was forbidden, so I never got the chance to meet 'real' people, workers, grafters, bakers, savour the tastes of foods from other countries, or witness entertainment that was frequent in our cities grand opera houses and theatres; I was kept safe away from the world, like a caged animal, Raven has shown me kindness and I have seen part of the world in its cruellest state, it's frightening, but it's real, far away from the hours of doll houses, pony rides and tea parties I was forced to attend.

A few days past, then a few weeks and I was effectively on the run, no word from my Father, whether he was still alive I don't know, Raven has kept very quiet on that subject, but no one else seems to have been looking for me.

Over the course of two weeks, I have seen a play in the local theatre, drank alcohol in a local tavern, dressed in normal clothes, a well welcomed relief from my royal gowns, corsets and hosiery; Raven has been showing me things that I had only heard about, he has opened my eyes to life and, I like it, I like it a lot.

One afternoon, we were hiding out in a small housing building, several rooms were here and were rented out to the highest bidder, the land-lady seemed nice, she slaved over the kitchen stove for several hours tending to the meat she had put on the boil for the many guests she had to feed, including me and Raven, whom I know from experience can really eat, that evening, over the table, he looked at me, that frown digging into his forehead when he asked.

"Princess what's wrong?" he asked, looking at me with worried eyes, he could see I was in more pain then I could tell him.

"Please … call me Caroline … it's just that … well, even being in a privileged family of royalty, I have never felt so, relevant or important to someone, you protect me like a prized possession, you've even put your life in danger to save me … even my Father, the King, hasn't done that, he would just lock me in my bed quarters, alone" I sigh, the realisation of my words sinking in, leaving a deep pit in my stomach.

"Never before have I felt so ... alive ...than in these past few days with you, you've shown me so much, I was always so sheltered, to an extent that I've not felt or experienced anything quite like this, being known by my subjects yet, so ignored at the same time, like some sort of porcelain doll no one can touch, it's heart-breaking, take me out of my fancy clothes into everyday ones that normal woman wear and no one has even recognised me, I had been made to be so ... elusive" I croak, feeling my throat grow thick as I fight back tears.

Raven frowns, reaching his hand to sit atop mine, he rises from his seat, ignoring everyone else in the dining area of the houses, making his way round to perch down in front of me.

"Have you ever been kissed by a man?" he asked me as I feel a crimson blush wash over me as I shook my head, looking down at the floor as I suddenly feel ashamed, thinking that Raven will think me immature, much to my surprize, he raises his hand to stroke my cheek.

"I'm glad, it means that no man has ruined your expectations of romance, I may be of the barbarian tribe and certainly am in appearance ... but I hope you know that I mean you no harm Princess, I feel as though I need to take a vow, as I am constantly overwhelmed by my need to protect you, my brothers will come looking for me so I may be gone for a while, but I will come back to you, you have my word on that …" he began, the feel of his scarred hand stroking my cheek sent shivers through me as I looked into his dark eyes.

"It may not be protocol Prin … Caroline …" he began, correcting himself by using my actual name to my delight as I smile.

"We are passed protocols now wouldn't you say … so please don't let this be a reflection of the act alone, I can assure you there is much more to this" he whispered, as I felt his lips on mine, gently pressing them against me in a soft kiss, sending shivers down my spine as I'd never been kissed before, especially by a man who was originally destined to kill me.

The next morning I wake from a blissful sleep, only to find that Raven has gone, the curtains sprayed open, spiralling in the wind as I leapt from the bed to look down from the balcony, he did say he would go, I thought to myself, feeling my eyes well up, I look away as my eyes fall upon a note placed on my bedside table, picking it up, tears now flowing freely down my cheeks, I read,

You may have been sheltered Princess, but it has not silenced your spirit, your courage or your passion, don't ever let that die, I have a duty to you, to keep you safe, I have gone back to my brothers, to make believe that all of the towns people have been slayed by my hand, at least then I know I can return to you without any followers, I will be with you soon, Princess,

Raven

Reading the note I find myself curled up on the floor as tears overwhelm me, I slept so well that, I don't know how long he's been gone and I have no way of knowing when he'll be back, the thoughts of the medieval torture he could be enduring if his brothers suspect he is lying filled me with dread as I felt my stomach tighten, all I can do is trust in his words, until my Raven returns to me. Suddenly my gaze falls upon a circlar object on the end of my bed, on closer inspection, I see it is a shield, attached to it, I see another small note.

Caroline ... this is for you, it was mine when I was training in battles, it is forced from strong metal and will protect you should you need it, but, also see the letters etched into it my love, this is the date I will return to you

Raven

Suddenly I notice some lettering reads: July 3rd, suddenly I feel a jolt in my stomach, that is tomorrow!

Later that day, I feel tears come over me thinking he may not return, it is quarter to midnight and there is no sign of him.

"Caroline …" says a voice as I turn to see Raven standing in my balcony as I run to him, his arms wrapping around my waist.

"My Princess" he says as he leans down to kiss me.

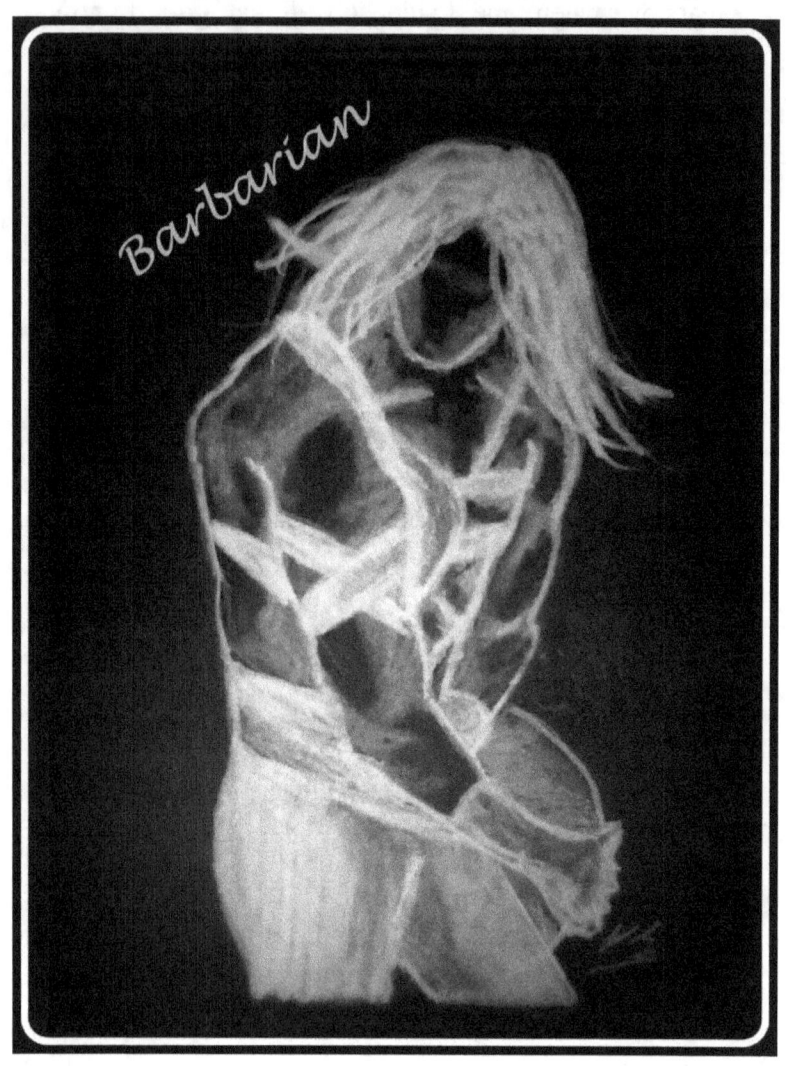

Barbarian

VAMPIRE'S REIGN

Much can be said about the vampire Princess, tales of her existence in central Europe date back centuries, sealed in time in the scriptures later told in the famous ghost stories you know of today, but none of them, tell of the truth behind this feared Princess.

The tale of a young, whole-hearted woman, taken by a vampire in the night and destined to do his bidding and roam the earth undead, leeching on mortals, sound a familiar tale?

Well, this is a slightly different tale, for the young woman in question was not destined to be an object for male fantasy or their faithful servant, in fact, she ruled over them, slayed those who threatened her strength, she was nothing short of a warrior goddess in her time, let me take you back, back into the time she was ruler of all she laid her eyes on, this is the story of the Vampire's reign.

Born into a family of crime and debauchery, Elizabeth was certain of many things, she could not trust anyone, steal from anyone or bargain with anyone. Until one day she met a man in the cities market, a curious soul with not but a cane and cloak to define him from the other moth eaten cretins of men she had met so far on this hot, muddy day in India where she had travelled to.

She found herself drawn to this dark stranger, upon greeting him, his skin pale as the snow of the mountains in China, eyes as deep as the sea she used to bathe in, offering her food from his trolley, they got talking of the adventures he had been on, travels to far away countries, witness to fame and fortune, mesmerised by his stories and with nowhere else to go, accept back to the hell she called home, she asked to go with him, so she too could see the world, meet new people and live.

Much to her surprize he agreed, with a smile as wide as the Nile, taking her arm he lead them back to his house, grand and old as she stood, gazing in glory as to its magnitude and wonder.

In the early hours she awoke from a dream, a nightmare, where she was in great pain, shaking and writhing with the new man at her side who mopped her sweaty brow, blood soaked was her pillow as she screamed in agony, begging for a release from this pain, her skin burning hot, her vision blurred, then, she suddenly woke up, to see the room she had fallen asleep in. The man had lent her his spare sleeping quarters, getting out of bed she walked to the mirror, stood dead still as she noticed two small markings on her neck, they looked like bites, mosquitoes? She thought to herself puzzled.

On closer inspection she saw a slight hint of a red trail from them, did she catch herself and bleed earlier, she thought? Suddenly she spotted the man out of the corner of her eye as she turned to look at him, who was smiling broadly at her.

"Now you will see the world for how it truly is … how do you feel Elizabeth?" he asked as she looked at him puzzled, her mouth slack,

"I don't understand" she said softly, her voice laced with fear as she turned back to the mirror, seeing the man had completely vanished, she darted back around to see him still stood behind her, yet he had no reflection, suddenly she began to feel very scared as she swallowed hard, her throat tight and dry.

"Who … what are you?" she asked, he laughed, a sickening sound that made her skin crawl as she felt her heart pound in her chest.

"This is life, you belong to me now Elizabeth, for eternity, let me show you what strength is!" he said as he reached for her, placing his strong grip on her shoulder in a move to pull her to him, she raised her hand onto his, as hard as she could and with a force she wasn't aware of, she threw him off of her, casting him aside like a ragdoll as his back hit the wall with a loud crash as the table smashed into pieces around him.

"DO NOT TOUCH ME!" she hollered, her chest heaving as she walked towards him, no longer scared as she stared down at him,

"Good God what have I turned you into!" he muttered as he clambered to his feet, clearly shaken as he held his lower back as he winced in pain.

"You are no partner for me as I had planned … the curse of the goddess … they said it was in this century that it would occur … this is … it must be … this is it … you are it … my god, the warrior vampire from the legend … it is …A woman!" he whispered in shock as he stared at her.

"Please … do not hurt me, I will do your bidding mistress, I swear, just please …" he said, crashing to his knees before her as she looked over her shoulder into the mirror, she saw a broader, bustier, more vibrate version of herself staring back at her, her rags of clothes now strong armour that curved to her shape.

"What the …" she muttered, running her hands over her form in disbelief.

"It was said that in a magic unknown to us, one day a person would be taken, willingly and upon this time, this change from mortality to immortality, a warrior would be born, a person more powerful than any other immortal known to man, this person could lead battles, bring peace or war to the world … this warrior … is you mistress … forgive me to bringing about this change in you but I did not know" he said, raising his hands in a gesture of surrender.

"The next time you step into the light, you will feel its burn unlike anything you've ever endured before, with your power, means you can withstand it for several hours before it becomes unbearable, unlike many others of your kind who may instantly turn into dust at the smallest glimpse of sunlight, but trust me Mistress, you will soon rule over much of this land and its people" he explained, slowly rising from his knees.

Elizabeth grew very weary of the man's tale, trying to ignore the ever growing pole of power she could feel surging through her very skin; this was nonsense, she thought to herself, when suddenly her arms grew thicker before her very eyes, expanding like a balloon, covered in armour glistening gold covering each knee, her breasts becoming bustier and her waist thicker, her hair growing by the second as she screamed in fear, when suddenly her eyes grew large as they bulged, as she tasted the sharp tang of her blood fill her mouth as she pricked her tongue with her new shining incisors, she turned to glimpse in the mirror once more, to see fangs staring back at her.

"What am I ... some sort of vampire warrior freak!" she cried,

"Yes Mistress, that's exactly what you are, well, minus the freak part of that statement ... you will be the fear of all who cross you, you have power that you have yet to realise, you are glorious to behold!" he exclaimed, bowing his head slightly forward.

"I will be at your service whenever you require Mistress" he added with a smile.

≈

That evening I go to bed in a hot sweat, I am assured that this is still part of the transformation as I toss and turn, in an uncomfortable heat as I am sponged down by my now male servant.

The next morning I feel alive, making my way straight to the mirror, the usual weathered looking young woman who used to stare back at me, now a distant memory, replaced a fully immersed structural face, my long hair perfect, shiny and placed as if it has been tended to for hours, my eyes sparkling with dark promise and a confident jaw that hides the sharp teeth that could silence anyone who were to question me, never before has I seen myself in such a way.

Suddenly, I see the sun creeping in across the carpet, moving over to the window I emerge into the midday suns glow, to feel a tickling sensation ripple over my skin, seeing a thin mist rise from my arms, am I burning?

"Your skin is sensitive to the sun Elizabeth, as I said to you, you can withstand it, but only for a few hours before you will become weary and your skin will need to rejuvenate, rather snakelike, you will need to shed layers of your skin which have been emerged in the suns strong rays for too long, do not fret mistress, it is normal for you, your people already know of your presence, the next time you step foot out of these four walls, you will find they will bow before you, this is your power mistress" he explained, bringing before me a platter of meats, cured and raw?

"You expect me to eat this? It's RAW your imbecile!" I scream at him, reaching for it and tossing it far across the room in a force that takes over without my consent, the rage frightens me as I come to my senses and suddenly recoil.

"Oh … I'm so sorry, I didn't mean to" I say, worrying as I reach to help him pick up the food, the floor now stained from the mess I have made, suddenly I am taken aback by the scent, feeling my nostrils flare.

"What is this madness?" I whisper.

"This is why I brought it to you mistress, you will soon begin to crave blood, at this stage, this rare steak and cured meats should suffice" he says as I reach for it like a magpie to a shiny object. Feeling it touch my lips I am filled with excitement, taking it between my teeth as I gnaw on it like a wild animal who had been starved for days, I begin to realise that I am no longer a woman, but a monstrous creature, no doubt capable of unspeakable things when my rage takes over.

The next few days and I begin to feel more and more of myself being replaced with this, animal instinct and warrior fighter that has replaced the once timid, adventurous soul that I called Elizabeth, my maker has decided that I need a new title, one that will strike fear into the hearts of my people, to ensure they do not question my power or become my enemies, he had spent many hours training me how to use a sword and to ride a horse.

A week later and he brings me a large, heavy object, seemingly so by the way he struggled to carry it as he walked with his back arched, as he strained to hold it up above his knees.

"This, mistress … is your shield … it has been in my family for centuries as I told you of this calling, I never believed that I would be the creator of such a marvel of female strength but I am mesmerized by it, this … is forged from the purest iron, embedded with platinum and is said to hold great power, you are to hold this in your right hand whilst mounting and riding your stallion horse, it was used in battle by our first warrior goddess, many centuries ago, she reigned for over a century and slayed any man who questioned her in battle, she made many of them her slaves, you are destined for greatness my mistress" he said, kneeling before me as he handed me the shield, taking it in my hand, I feel no weight to it as its handle fits perfectly around my fist as I hold it up, admiring the craftsmanship.

Then, I hear a bang on the downstairs doors as my maker turns his head, beads of sweat forming on his brow as he turns back to look at me, fear in his eye.

I feel it, a deep, dark swarm swirling in the pit of my stomach, rising up like a furnace, as I reach for the door of my chambers, leaving my maker behind and make my way downstairs.

Opening the door on this hot day in India, I find two men before me, one small, bald headed man, wrapped in what looked like a large brown blanket and the other man stood proudly in front of him, tall, muscular, with long dark hair tied back, his eyes dark with a grin that urged me to slap it off of him.

"Aww … so this is the glorious warrior goddess we have been told so much about … aww … she's smaller than I thought, not exactly the amazon of your ancestors are you pretty lady … perhaps you should get your master to undo this change, it doesn't become you … your hair too … pruned … your body … too small and meek looking … go back to your travelling little girl … let the men rule this earth, not the sewing, tea-making girls like yourself!" he whispered, his grin never leaving his smug face.

Each word, fuelling my wrath further as I smile sweetly at him, bringing my shield before him as I detect a flicker of fear in his eyes as I reach back my arm and force it forward, landing my fist straight into his stomach, propelling him backwards off of the porch, over the steps and onto the pebbled ground about fifteen feet away from my feet.

"YOU DARE QUESTION ME! … you arrogant, bumbling, cretin … you tell your other … weak, excuses for men that you are no match for this power … If you dare question me again, I will see to it that all of their heads be paraded on their own swords … oh … and my name is not girl, or lady … tell your boys that Lewella sends her greetings won't you … you poor excuse for a warrior, you are nothing more than the devils smile and bulls bollocks … you are nothing but a sick animal who craves attention by men weaker than yourself … go back home little boy … go play with your toy soldiers … they are as close as you will ever get to fighting like a MAN! I screamed at him, each word spat like pure venom as he cowered back from me, rising from his feet, himself and the small man ran off, faster than my eyes could keep up.

Each day that passed, I grew stronger, the battle cries and techniques taught to me by my maker all seemed to come naturally with little, if no effort at all, I could see now that everything I had been expected to be, was indeed coming to its head, ready to be put into practice as the town grew restless with no sight of me to prove the promising rumours.

Soon it became time, the Government had been turned over, the high class families moved out of harm's way and all that lay before me was the promise of a mighty battle, scenes of disarray in the streets below the window to which I first witnessed my bodies new reaction to sunlight, each night drew more of the immortal, leeching monsters that I was claimed to be a part of, connected too and to rule over as my maker explained.

Each night, I would hear the cries of innocent people, fallen prey to the cunning and hypnotising powers of my immortal subjects, all servants of the monstrous nature that had claimed their mortality, leaving them empty, blood thirsty shells, it was my duty to restrain them, to let them know that they could not prey freely, but at my command and on those who were riddling this place with criminal and immoral activity, those such souls I would condone to such a fate as death, the innocent ones must be spared.

The next evening, I made my way to the Government grand hall, riding in on horseback with my sword and shield in hand as my mighty stallion carried me there swiftly.

Finding the throne my maker had informed me of, I took my seat, the cushioned padding bracing my back, as I placed my sword in the handle, a perfect fit and my shield braced on the iron bracket, just like my maker had instructed. My eyes found the next challenge, a large, speaker, a fanned out tulip design; I took it in my hands, my maker told me that not many females could lift the object as it was made from pure iron and marble, alas, It felt like mere small weights to my strong arms which pulsated as I brought it close to my lips.

"This is your warrior, your ruler, Lewella … I am the embodiment of the stories you have all been fed these last few days, I can assure your safety, if you comply with the simple rulings of my nature, in the spirit and respect of my ancestors who all bravely fought for your rights in this land, I reign next in line … and take my place at the rightful head of this council … there are immortals amongst us, myself included, I will see to it that all who prey of innocent lives, will be taken … any immortal acts I see as unjustified will be swiftly dealt with … by me … heed this and I will do you no harm … but a warning … any man who dare cross me or question my rightful place here … before you as your protector, will be … silenced" I say in a voice I am still becoming accustomed to as the speaker bellows out my statement to all in the land, my highly sensitive hearing picking up on the many cheers of my followers and hateful laughter of my soon to be enemies.

All there is to do now, is sit and savour the glory in the power I now behold, in the hope that it can be used for the greater good, as I now sit proudly where my ancestors sat, now, I begin, my vampires reign.

Vampires
Reign

ICE TEARS

During a long blisteringly cold winter, a young woman got caught in a blizzard, with only her cape to cover her clothes to shelter her, she took hiding under a large oak tree, it was said that there, she froze. Soon, she became a mark for tourists who had heard of the ice girl who had been frozen in time and believed this to be a sign of great power, people would travel far and wide to tell her their secrets and make wishes before her feet, each Christmas Eve she would come to life, taking shelter in an old bare cabin in the forest surrounded by trees and woodland creatures, it is here she could grant the wishes given to her by passers-by earlier that year.

Every so often, she would get a wish from an unfortunate, saddened soul, wishing for food, shelter or good health, it is these whom she granted much grand things, as they would not ask for more than their most simple needs.

When word travelled back to her by the flying creatures, of the granted wishes she had cast, she would shed tears of happiness, ice tears, tears that were said to hold snowflakes within them, as they would trail down to the poor children in the land, it is these tears that showed travellers of her power, she was made from the freak nature of our forever changing seasons and was granted with a power that changed so many, she soon became known as the Magical Ice Princess with magical Ice Tears.

The reign of this ice girl was quite the spectacle, as even in the warmest of evenings and blisteringly hot days of summer, she did not melt, not a drop from her icy form would touch the soiled ground, a spell from the gods, it was believed, was the reason for this strange phenomenon, people were told to keep away every December the 24th, as not to tamper with such a special event, it was not a simple transformation for her to form movement, still a solid piece of ice, yet able to walk and move freely for one night only, at precisely 7pm you could hear the faint hum from her lips as her soul began to come to life, humming tunes she had heard all year, within minutes each limb would become mobile, once her feet became free she would dance, parading through the trees like a kid in a candy store racing for the front door. On the search for the cabin she was welcomed by the woodland creatures who scattered around the cabin entrance, bowing their heads in acceptance and praise as she patted each one on the head as they followed her into the cabin whose door had magically opened at the swish movement of her glistening hand.

Settling down on the nearby stool, she closed her eyes, her mind flooding with the wishes she had carried all year as she began to shift through them to make her decisions on who was worthy of their wishes being granted, the poor families always came first, as they asked for the least, one young boy came to mind, who she recalled stood before her shaking from her cold form or fear she did not know, but his words sunk into her like no one else's had.

"Please mam … I'm Tommy … I'm seven and my Ma has been taken ill, I don't know what type of wish you can grant but I know you are magic, could you make her better, we don't have much food and the rood blew off of our home in the storm last month but please make her better, my Daddy went away and hasn't come back … please make my Mummy better ice princess … thank you" he whispered, his voice soft and gentle like his demeanour, taking a deep breath in, she hummed a tone, as flashes of the boy's face came across her mind as she granted his wish, although he didn't ask for anything more, her lips perked up in a soft smile as she asked the powers to fix the roof and allow for food to come to the boys reach, suddenly a glimpse of the boy smiling, tears of joy running down his face as he hugged his Mother close to him, the ice princess smiled, a warm sensation flooding across her heart as she knew the wish had reached them.

Ice Tears

THE BAT, THAT SAT

In a cave, off of the edge of a cliff in Pennsylvania, lived a coven of bats, all identical, all accept for one, he was not exceptional in his appearance, size or colour, as he sported the same black long ears and long wings as his brothers, but what made him truly unique was that he, unlike the others, did not hang upside down, he was the only bat to see the world for all its misshapen glory, for he sat upright, walked and even slept up the right way.

Each winter, when it grew dark and gloomy, the bats would take flight, over the heads of onlookers who mistook them for birds, these mysterious creatures flew on the call from the wolves of the night, who howled at the ever brightening full moons that highlighted the midnight sky, these calls summoned the bats to their maker, the feared and solitary vampire who lived in the adjoining caves, alone and just awakened from a long sleep in his coffin, decked with the finest red velvet and silks, like a dog is man's best friend, the bats would do the bidding of their master, following the wolves howl to lead them to the vampires location.

Upon their swoop, he would stroke their wings as they settled around the edge of the antique wood and gold that braced his coffin, he would silently tell them of the places they must go and the women they must bring to him, as he had been alone for many decades now and in his weakened state of awake he had not fed, it was this, that the bats granted him, all accept, the bat who sat upright, for he could not fly the same lengths as his brothers, he became the onlooker for his siblings, watching the night sky for changes, that would be for him to signal their safe return before daylight called.

This job made this rather special bat known by all manner of other creatures and soon, he became trusted by the wolves, bears and even lions in faraway lands.

Their master was granted many willing subjects, women, brought to him by many a route, some by carriage, some by flight, some travelled of their own means, happy in their trance like state before their fate was sealed.

The bat that sat, soon became known in many lands, cities and caves and lived to be the successor of his brothers, for it became known that they all ceased to be, due to the blood rushing circumstances that made them hang upside down, the bat that sat was spared this fate, therefore, his master was never alone for long.

The Bat
that Sat

THE ROSE SANCTUARY

On the grounds of a great mansion, was a beautiful rose garden, with every type of rose you could think of, every colour, every hue, it was soon called the rose sanctuary. It was said that at night, the rose garden was tended to by the ghosts of the mansions ancestors, so that each morning when the gardener arrived, he would come to find that the roses had all been magically pruned and fed.

Until one year, nothing bloomed, as the house learned that its master had been brutally murdered in the mansions grounds, a deep sadness covered the area and all the roses in his masters garden wilted overnight, beautiful blooms now a distant memory, this went on for the twelve months that the family mourned, no amount of pruning, watering or feed brought the roses back, even the night ghosts were in mourning as they did not have the heart to touch the once luscious blooms.

One crisp morning, the sky was littered with the sounds of distant cries, many people had said they could hear the cries of a man, that echoed across the land and lead back to the mansion, the family couldn't bear to live in the mansion, so close to where their master, a husband, a brother, a father, a friend, had been killed, so on the eve of the last cry being heard, they left, taking their belongings to a nearby house until their lawyers had sorted out the scandal that surrounded them and their family as the murderer had never been caught.

As for the rose sanctuary, it was said that as the master laid amongst the shrubbery on the night he was killed, a single cut rose had been placed in his hand as he lay motionless, it is this that was believed to be the reason why even the mansions grounds were also in mourning.

One crisp, cold morning in September, a frost set in, covering the leaves yellow grass in its light white hue, the gardener arrived to cut down the remaining rose bush under instruction from the masters wife; every step resonated with the crunch of footsteps from the gardeners large brown boots. After pruning the hedge which stood a large structure of twigs, he left, turning once more to see the now dark and gloomy garden; suddenly, the ancestors ghosts appeared before him.

The man stumbled backwards, tripping over his own feet and landing hard on the icy ground, raising his finger to point at them, they looked at each other with small smiles.

"Who … are you … what … what?" the gardener stuttered, trembling in fear as he looked straight through them.

"Do not fear … cast your mind back to the old portraits on the master's library walls and you may recall our faces are familiar to you" the woman said, moving slightly closer to the man who sat motionless as his breathing started to regulate.

"The masters Great-Grandparents, Martha and … Thomas … really? How is that possible, you two both …" he began, now moving to his feet as his legs shook.

"Died … yes it's true, we died many years ago, but we have been back here ever since, to watch over our Great-Grandson, since you are the only person still returning to these grounds then we have to tell our knowledge to you … we know who took him from us, his murderer" said Thomas, as the gardener frowned slightly, now standing directly in front of the ghostly couple.

"What is your name?" Martha asked, stepping to stand directly in front of him.

"Edward … I'm the gardener here, have been for forty three years" he said, "You say you know who murdered the master?" he added.

The couple looked at each other, lowering their heads as Thomas moved beside Edward.

"I don't know how much you know about the family Edward, but let us take a walk, this may take some time to explain" Thomas began, as they started to walk around the grounds.

"This family goes back many generations, the rose sanctuary gets its name from my wife, she used to prune it whilst pregnant with our first child, she found it comforted her, she would sit out here every day, rain or shine and it became her sanctuary … many years past and our Great Grandson came along, now with offspring of his own who would take on the mansions heritage like I once did, but there is much corruption in this family Edward … the master had grown old and weary and had amounted such an empire that it widely was known of his wealth, I'm sad to tell you that he was killed by someone very close to him, so close that he probably didn't see it coming, his eldest Son!" Thomas said, each word spoken with a heavy heart, Edward stopped, looking at the couple and shook his head, his eye blazed with anger and confusion.

"His own boy, Tommy! Named after yourself, don't be absurd … why? This doesn't make any sense" he said, now pacing.

"I know, but we saw it happen right over there, Tommy was due to take his father's fortune until his baby Sister arrived 6 months ago, you must know of the new will that the master had drawn up with his lawyer, him and his wife had always wanted a little girl and it was said that if a girl was to be born, she would inherit the fortune, as so many men had inherited the families fortune before and often squandered, he had hoped that a change of terms may bring the future of their family better fortune if a lady was to be master of the mansion … of course Tommy was furious when he learned of this and I'm afraid … that is why the master is now dead, shot, with the masters own gun … it is very sad" Martha continued, wiping a tear off of her translucent face.

"Well this isn't good enough, Tommy is with the rest of the family now … I must tell someone" the gardener cried, seeing the ghosts vanish into smoke, he turned and made his way for the nearby town.

Taking a carriage to the town, the gardener called after the master's wife Emily, reaching her, he held both her arms with urgency as she looked at him with a startled expression, clutching her young daughter's blanket.

"Mam ... I must speak with you … I know who killed the master … I have proof ... Please... come with me its urgent man … please … this way" Edward said, Emily, seeing the desperation in the gardener's eyes followed him without question, and they climbed into the carriage and made their way back to the mansions grounds.

"You've heard of Martha and Thomas correct?" Edward Askes, to which she nodded her head slowly.

"Well … I think they can tell you more" he continued, stepping out of the carriage and helping her as her leather boots made contact with rose sanctuary once more, she took a deep breath as tears began to flow freely down her porcelain cheeks, clutching her stomach which rumbled as she'd barely been able to eat a full meal in recent weeks since her husband's death.

"Thomas!!! …. Martha, are you there?" Edward called, walking down the small pathway, once surrounded by bright pink roses, now a mass of wood and vine.

Suddenly Emily turned, to see the ghost of Thomas, as she screamed, falling back onto Edward who luckily caught her before she hit the hard ground, she stared at them, shocked as her jaw became slack as she struggled to form words.

"Please … don't try to speak dear lady … just listen instead … this will be very heard to hear" Thomas began as Martha walked up beside him, placing her hand on his shoulder as Emily could see her hand through Thomas's back.

A light blue haze surrounded the ghostly couple, with a translucency that allowed you to see through them, but apart from that, they looked quite real, Emily took a deep breath, clutching her arm around her small frame to sooth her shivering as the ghosts explained.

Emily screamed as she heard the verdict of her eldest son's actions, disbelief and denial as she cursed the ghosts for making up such outlandish tales of rubbish, but, she was soon silent when they showed her the scene of the crime to which Edward had to calm her.

Once month later, the truth had been told and Tommy, the eldest boy had been looked away in the nearby prisoners tower for his crimes after confessing. With the truth known and her husband's soul free, the rose garden miraculously came into bloom, more vibrate than ever before, the gardener need not tend to it as it appeared to self-sustain to the families disbelief, Edward was made a butler in the household, a title he took with pride and all was well.

It was also said that on occasion, echoes of a man's laugh could be heard on the wind and a few sightings had been reported of a man walking the mansions grounds, admiring the roses, clutching one single cut rose in his hand.

Rose Sanctuary

HEARTBREAK TOWER

"In heartbreak creek, there lived five fat trolls, five fat trolls had seven skinny moles, seven skinny moles had three green hats, three green hats fashioned two black bats, two black bats flew to heartbreak tower and on this tower we begin our tale … told … on the hour" said the old man to the neighbour children, who would travel far and wide with their families to hear such stories from the old man in heartbreak tower.

The tower sat proud near a small creek just south of the main river. Towering above all nesting trees, the old man who lived there could gaze down upon the little village, two shops, one post office and one doctor's surgery and the main hall made up the small street with locals nestled behind or above the shops.

It was said that the old man had lived there all his life, man and boy, on his 80th birthday he came out of hiding and made his way to the town's main hall to tell the neighbourhood children tales of his life and dreams, stories of the creek monsters and the towers ghosts soon became a tradition in the small town and every Halloween the children and their families would make their way to the tower to visit the old man and hear his ghost stories.

Oct 31st 1925, the old man set the scene, in the top of the tower where the best sights could be seen, he would place small log stools he had carved many moons ago as a young man, resting them neatly in a circle ready for the children to take their seats.

The room soon was crowded and the wind could be heard howling through the windows thin pane of glass, the children huddled around with cups of hot chocolate in hand, their parents sat on the large benches behind, waiting for the old man to appear.

Every Halloween, like clockwork, the man would appear at precisely 8.08pm, as he believed this time symbolized the story of the snakes that existed in his annual first story, for the shape of the number 8 twisted and turned like the venomous sliders, the man would reveal more from the slithery creatures story each year and the children, usually running wild and free, climbing trees and playing tag, would sit in mesmerized silence for over an hour listening intently to the man's tales.

He would tell of stories of famous boats that were haunted with the spirits of men lost at sea and a talking ships carving of a lady at the helm; tales of witches who would tire aimlessly to cast a spell to cure their bad fortune of undesirable faces. Then, he would tell of the ghost who was reported to be seen riding his mighty steed into the darkness, reliving the last battle in which he fought, before he and his horse passed on.

Although the children loved to hear the man's stories, no one knew of the true horror he had experienced, as half of the stories he told, were in fact, true.

Many years the old man was in isolation, as he kept away from sight for several years, vowing never to repeat the things he had seen, until one morning over his daily cereal, he was visited by the ghost of his friend in battle; a great war the families had started, the old man lost his friend and his horse in battle, the ghost spoke to him, saying for him to not hide, but to share the experiences with the world in his memory. From that day he has done just that and since that day, he was no longer plagued by nightmares from his past.

Every night while the old man slept he would dream of such times, though they no longer haunted him, he made sure those experiences would never be in vain.

After the night of stories, everyone left the tower, leaving the old man to his thoughts as he began to clear the room of seats and cups. Suddenly the man heard a voice, seeming to be coming from the top tower, the old man turned towards it and began to follow the sound.

"Benjy …. Benjy …" said the voice, in a soft, high pitched singsong tone.

Following the voice up the spiral staircase, lead the old man to the top tower, a space he hadn't been in for many years, his ears filled with the sounds of a voice he knew, his younger Sister, who was playing in the tower when they were children, she tripped and fell out of the window, she didn't make it, but he was haunted with the memory of that day ever since, it inspired the story 'Girl in the grass' which he attempted to tell each year but couldn't bring himself to do it, for the shame it brought him, he had always blamed himself, thinking he could've done something to save her.

Since that night, he had heard her voice every so often, the tower was haunted by her tones, and he left that part for the tower unattended for decades until this night, the room that inspired the name 'Heartbreak Tower'.

"Benjy ... come and play" said the voice, the old man felt tears spring to his eyes at the sweet voice he thought he'd forgotten after so many years, turning suddenly to make his way downstairs he stopped, his feet felt heavy, weighed down to the ground.

There before him, was the ghost of his little Sister, her hair in pigtails, her usual cheery smile on her face, holding a skipping robe.

"Benjy ... please don't be sad, It's ok, I'm fine, you don't tell the children about me and I don't know why ... what's wrong?" she says as the old man smiles softly, wiping away the tears with the back of his hand.

"I want you to tell them the story of me Benjy ... I'm still here and I'm fine ... I listen to your stories with the other children, you tell them so well" says the little girl with a spring in her step.

The old man nods his head but doesn't utter a word, he simply smiles, and then, just as quickly as she appeared, she vanishes, leaving a giggle in her place as the old man laughs in joy, for the first time in years, he was free.

Heartbreak Tower

THE MAZE

In an old Victorian house, lived the largest grounds in Great Britain, for many years, several gardeners were hired to prune its wild nature, as the houses owner would insist on harsh pruning to tame the grounds unruly determination to take over and strangle any other plants in its way.

Until, illness took several of the men away from their gardening duties, a thick lush green began to grow confidently high above the ground, soon enough, thick black vines grew, twisting and turning in all directions, soon the grounds were to be unrecognisable.

One morning the butler rose at dawn, dressing himself in his fine attire, his full length mirror ensuring that his tie was straight; out of the corner of his eye he caught a glimpse of the garden, gasping in shock, his eyes landed upon a large labyrinth, a maze of hidden corners, curved alleys and twisted thorns surrounded in a thin mist.

"Oh my goodness" said the butler, his voice echoing the shock before his eyes. Quickly, the butler made his way from his room, sprinting down the staircase as fast as his long lean legs could carry him, making his way to the masters study to make his announcement known; his master looked up from over his half-moon spectacles, with a look of confusion across his brow, as to the reason to his butlers sudden dishevelled appearance.

"Sir … if you please … there is a problem … outside, the garden is, has … changed Sir … please … you must look" says the butler, his voice shaky as the master makes his way around his large desk to follow the butler outside.

The Master stops short as soon as his face hits the fresh air, several leaves pooling around his feet adorned with his library slippers, stood there in shock; slowly his head moved upwards towards the sky, following the large obstacle that was before him.

"Steven … what is this madness, I saw the grounds only yesterday afternoon, what is this?" the master said, looking troubled at his butler who shook his head, seemingly just as baffled by the sight.

"I do not know Sir … I only noticed it seconds before I came to find you … it seems to have grown overnight … what could this mean?" Steven asked, turning his head back to the overgrown maze as a mist slowly began to circle their feet.

There, surrounded by thousands of tiny leaves that were blowing in the breeze, stood a grand sight indeed, a labyrinth, a maze unlike anything the master had laid his eyes on, there was one other he knew of in Europe, that was said to have sprung up from nowhere overnight, it was said to be due to a curse deep underground, the master immediately ran inside back to his study and put his hands on his red leather phone book and quickly reached for the phone, dialing in the numbers he was put through to a dear friend he saw once a year at the grand ball every New Year's Eve, a friend that new well of this legend.

Steven took a step outside again, as the mist had mysteriously lifted, walking towards it he began to walk towards the mazes opening, only to hear the voice of his master in the distance calling him back inside.

"Steven … you fool … get back here … it's not safe!" called the master, still clinging to the end of the phone as he peered out of the nearby window at Steven who kept on walking at an alarmingly slow yet steady pace, not his usual walk at all, it was almost trance like, before too long the master began to feel very uneasy looking at Steven in the distance when suddenly, the maze moved, followed by a nearby branch reaching out and pulling him in.

"STEVEN!" the master called, dropping the phone cord and standing at the door looking on, there before him, was Steven, his usual smart self, stood perfectly still and proud with one hand held behind his back, only, encased in green leaves and vines, the perfect statue of Steven has been cast by the maze, no sign of the real Steven to be found.

The master gasped in fear as he stared upon the perfectly formed garden sculpture of his once faithful butler, he ran back inside and hollered down the phone to his friend, his voice a mixture of fear and anger as he spat out his words in a plea.

The next morning, the master was awakened by the sound of a horse and cart drawing up outside his mansion, as he leaped out of bed and stood in front of his bedroom window, the sounds of the horse's hooves clipping the stone ground in front of the giant labyrinth.

The Master scurried out of bed, grabbing his dress robe, slippers and quickly made his way down the stairs to open the door.

There in front of him stood his old friend and famed mystic Muriel Tookit, although they didn't speak more than once a year, they had known each-other since their days at College and she was after all, known for her many skills and talents and had helped many unfortunate people deal with a range of mystical and frightening circumstances, from poltergeists, moving furniture and strange voices, her skills had to help the Master out of his gardening issues, he hoped.

"Muriel ... thank you so much for coming so quickly at such short notice ... I really need your help, as you probably can tell, my problems are very close to home, the monstrous maze that has taken over my beautiful garden" explained the Master.

Muriel removed her black leather gloves and lowered her head as she placed them into her handbag, her wide brimmed hat fully covering her face as she bent forward slightly to step over the fresh-hold.

"Timothy, I'm very glad you called me …it may surprise you to know that yours is not the first call I've received on problems such as this, only a month ago … I had a call about another labyrinth that had sprung up from nowhere in someone's back garden … let us sit and I will explain more over a cup of tea" she explained, taking Timothy's hand in hers as she saw the worry in his eyes.

In his study they sat with cups of tea in hand, Muriel taking a biscuit as she began her story.

"Timothy … I have heard of a great sadness that comes over certain mystics once every decade, when one is cast into disgrace, there's a prophecy that states that it's this disgrace that changes the direction of any spell that's cast by a mystic, it started by a gardener who went to a mystic and asked for something to help his plants grow as they all died after the death of his beloved wife, the spell went array and since then, all gardens have been overcome with a large labyrinth type structure" she explained, sipping at her tea.

Timothy looked very confused as he leant forward slightly, trying to take it all in.

"But … I've had no problems with my garden, all the plants were fine, the trees too, I don't understand" he said, shaking his head.

"Well, if nothings affected your crops or plants, how about your staff, do you have gardeners?" Muriel asked, setting the cup down on the table beside her.

"Err, well yes actually, I have several … as it's such a large garden, and actually … most of my gardeners have been taken ill recently, all of them, accept my butler who didn't tend to the garden but is now part of it!" Timothy stated.

Muriel looked confused and smiled.

"A part of your garden, whatever do you mean?" she asked, chuckling slightly in confusion.

"The labyrinth, we were both stood near it and suddenly I saw him walking towards it, it was actually as I was on the phone to you … he just kept walking … and now he's … let me show you" he said, setting his cup down as he led her out towards the labyrinth as she cautiously followed him.

Then, before her, stood the large maze, although the sky above it held the morning sun and there wasn't a cloud in the sky, Muriel lowered her gaze upon the maze, she noticed that it held a dark mist around it, like smoke hiding a wealth of secrets.

She turned to Timothy and he raised his arm, extending his hand to point to the left of the labyrinth, Muriel's gaze fell upon the green statue of Steven, a collection of twisted thorns, thick brown vines and lush green leaves, making the perfect silhouette of the houses butler.

"This is more serious than I thought Timothy, would you mind if I made a phone call?" she asked, turning to him with a look of concern plastered across her porcelain skin. Timothy nodded in silence as she made her way inside, only to hear the sounds of the labyrinth behind her as she turned to see it moving from side to side, like a dance of the winds as leaves were swiftly blown around her, suddenly, a vine came out from no-where, grabbing her around the waist as she had no time to scream as it took her breath away, before pulling her sharply into its hedges.

"MURIEL!!" Timothy screamed after her as he began to follow her in until his senses took hold, not wanting to be taken in himself, he vaguely heard her voice call out to him.

"Timothy … call Derek, my address book, call Derek!" she called, before too long Timothy heard a rumbling sound, soon to be followed by the hedges parting, he squinted and saw the silhouette of Muriel carved in lush green foliage, every detail immaculate, even down to the details of her wide brimmed hat, the vines carefully curving to form the perfect shape.

Timothy felt an utter despair take over as he scurried inside to get Muriel's bag, pulling out an address book he quickly punched in the numbers into the phone.

"Derek … it's Timothy, I'm a friend of Muriel's, there has been a terrible curse over my mansion, Muriel has been taken, she told me to phone you" his voice a panic.

"Ahh, so it's true, what Muriel has been telling me of her recent findings, you are next to be plagued by the curse of the earth my poor unfortunate gentlemen, do not fret, meet me in the old part of town this evening, I may have some information that will help you, I was Muriel's predecessor, old in years but the mind is still very much intact, I taught her everything she knows, until tonight, 6.30pm, the tavern near the stream, do you know it?" asked the man as Timothy agreed, placing the phone back in its carrier, he took a deep breath, barricading himself inside until it was time for him to leave.

The horse and carriage drew up outside as he gingerly moved through the empty mansion, locking the door as he left and made his way into the carriage.

The long journey to the tavern, to meet with a stranger, his only hope was that this man could be trusted under the recommendations of Muriel, whom he trusted with his life.

It wasn't long before the carriage drew to a stop, the driver feeding the horses after their hour long journey and Timothy made his way into the tavern, with no idea what this man looked like, with only his name to go by, he made his way up to the barman.

"Excuse me Sir, is there a Derek in here somewhere?" he asked to the barman who was drying off some wine glasses before extending his arm over to the far right hand corner, Timothy turned to see an old man wrapped in a grey cape, adorning a hat and gloves.

"Excuse me … Derek?" Timothy asked, the old man raised his head and stood up, extending his gloved hand to him.

"Timothy, I've heard a lot about you from Muriel, I take it she has been possessed by some form of earthly curse am I right?" Derek asked as the men took their seats, the barman making his way over to them as they both ordered the house beer of tap.

"Yes, my garden has been taken over by a large labyrinth, it has completely engulfed everything, worst of all it has taken two people … my butler and now Muriel, I don't know where exactly they go, but all that is left is the perfect silhouette of them, like a cast sculpture, it is some black magic or something I am sure of it" Timothy explained with horror in his voice.

Derek listened, not a man of many words, taking a gulp of his beer, he began to explain,

"I don't know how much Muriel was able to tell you before she was taken but … It is to the best of my knowledge that such curses are spread across lands, gardens, such are common venues due to their nature of spreading around, like weeds, so, naturally, this is what has happened with you … I would say that, nearby somewhere, a curse was made and it has gradually grown into your land, the only way this can be reversed is to trace it back" said the old man.

"Trace it back? You mean I have to find out where the curse originally came from, that is impossible, it could be anywhere, anyone!" Timothy said in despair.

"For you yes Sir, for me, not so … I am gifted in these such ways, hence why Muriel came to me to learn the art, I would suggest that you take me to your mansion and I can explore the grounds, my skills will protect me from the curse engulfing me, Muriel's skills are, very new shall we say, mine are a bit more experienced … I will attempt to trace the curse outside of the grounds, this should give us a good chance of finding out where it started" explained the man, gulping yet more of his beer, seemingly calm in his demeanour.

Timothy looked at the man, slightly intrigued yet just as worried as he slowly nodded, at a loss for any other possible avenue to try, what did he have to lose?

"I would suggest you tell me all you know about the grounds heritage, who owned the land before yourself, its history, and any traumas or nearby struggles, this may give us a good starting point" Derek asked.

Timothy began to think back, there were many books of the mansions history in his study, perhaps there would a clue in there, he thought to himself.

"There has been many I believe, there was a great scandal a century ago which was quite famous, I don't know all the details but there was some discord in the family that lived in my mansion, a secret and some sort of disgrace occurred, part of the house was separated up and this caused a huge feud that carried on for decades, I don't know if it was ever solved, after that I don't know a great deal, I certainly wouldn't know about any of the other grounds nearby for I don't know anyone to that degree, beyond polite familiarity you understand" he explained as Derek simply nodded, listening intently.

"Well … may I suggest we start tracing back the steps, go back a few decades before you arrived in the mansion, these things are often old and can take years to take hold, I would imagine it has something to do with the land that the person lived on, rather than a curse just to an individual person, a curse to have this sort of magnitude sounds very much to me like it was cast by someone who wanted many people to pay, not just one" Derek added, draining his mug of beer before signalling the barkeep for another.

"Do you think it has something to do with the family before mine then?" Timothy asked, finishing his mug of beer.

"I cannot know for sure, but It certainly sounds likely, we must research more to be sure as I say … may I suggest we start tomorrow at dawn, this is when the curse will be at its weakest, then, I can search the grounds, night-time and dusk is when it's at its most deadly, it preys on loss of light, so sunlight will be our friend tomorrow, that and the hand of the Lord to watch over us" Derek said, starting his next mug of beer.

The following morning, Derek arrived at the crack of dawn, just as he had said, wrapped in the same grey cape and hat as he emerged from the carriage to greet Timothy who had a ghostly look on his face.

"My man you do not look well, has something else happened?" Derek enquired, seeing Timothy's white skin tone.

"No Derek, I just haven't been able to sleep since all this has happened, I do hope we will have some progress today, this is the front grounds as you can see and there, are the two silhouettes of my butler Steven and Muriel" Timothy said,

Pointing into the parted hedges as Derek slowly stepped forward, the hedges began to move slightly, to Timothy's dismay as he warned Derek, who simply raised his hand, the hedges did not move forward, or seem to make any attempt to take him as it had done to Steven and Muriel.

"As I told you yesterday Timothy, it cannot affect me, I know of a far greater power than this, God is watching over, so I have no fear of it ... the sculptures are merely made up of vine and foliage my good man ... there is no sign of human life inside them ... and ..." Derek began, now closing his eyes and breathing in deeply, stretching out his arms wide.

"They are not far, Steven and Muriel are alive, so no fears on that, we just need to locate them, which I'm sure will be revealed once we have determined where this curse orientated from, I'm actually feeling a strong pull from the mansion itself Timothy, would you mind if I took a look inside?" Derek asked, turning his back on the maze and stepping inside.

"So you don't think we have to actually follow the maze through then?" Timothy asked.

"Absolutely not, you would think that but no … that is the curses trap, it is designed to intrigue you so that you will step foot inside it, the reason Muriel and Steven were taken in the first place was just that, the labyrinth has great power Timothy, it sensed that they both wanted to enter it, but as they must have displayed some sort of hesitation, it took them anyway" Derek explained, as he and Timothy walked into the grand hall of the mansion, Derek walked slowly, taking everything in, pausing every so often to look more closely.

"Is there a particular part of this mansion that has been known to have held some sort of discord, perhaps an argument, fight or something like that" Derek asked.

"Actually yes, the basement was known to have been used as a disciplinary room from time to time, I believe that this was once used as a boarding school and also housed a rather dysfunctional family, the ones I told you of yesterday, the basement was used to correct people who were not deemed to be behaving" Timothy explained.

"Ah, well, that sounds like something that could have caused this … maybe it's not a curse as I thought, perhaps it's a spirit trying to send a message" Derek said as they made their way to the basement.

As Derek entered the basement, he began to shake, his body convulsing before quickly running out.

"Derek?" Timothy said, placing his hand on Derek's shoulder.

"I am certain, it is not a curse my dear man, it is a spirit, I can feel it, there is an abnormal chill surrounding that room, it is a woman, she is sending a message, the maze is a symbol of some kind … I must rest Timothy, I can feel myself weakening" he explained, leaning against the wall for support as Timothy led him back to the lounge and drew him some brandy to revive him.

"So you think it is a symbol you say?" Timothy asked, handing Derek the round bottomed glass.

Derek nodded slowly, taking a sip of the brandy.

"Yes … I do not know all yet … first I will rest, I do hope you will not object to myself staying the night, but I think I am close to solving this puzzle and that I will need tomorrow to continue" Derek said as Timothy agreed.

The following morning, Timothy woke to the smell of coffee brewing and the tinkling of his piano being played, making his way downstairs, to find Derek sat at the piano, playing a cheery tune, with a large mug of coffee beside him.

"Sleep well Derek?" Timothy enquired, making his way into the lounge to take a seat in his favourite armchair, cushioned seats sporting the shape of the man.

"Yes thank you Timothy, forgive me … I hope I did not disturb you?" Derek said in his usual calm tone as he slowly turned around on the stool to face him.

"No not at all, I was just waking up anyway … you were going to have a look around the grounds this morning?" Timothy asked as Derek got to his feet, placing his moth eaten hat on his head as he stood up straight.

Outside, the sun was just rising above the clouds, a light breeze lifting up the ends of Timothy's robe, yet the breeze did not touch any of the leaves of the maze that seemed to be getting bigger by the day.

"It is definably a symbol, I can feel it, it is linked to that young women somehow, I feel the same pull around it that I felt yesterday in the basement with her spirit" Derek said, before turning on his heel and heading back inside, Timothy stood, with a look of confusion on his face, before quickly following him.

"Forgive me Timothy, I have to find out more about the spirit of that women, it will provide the missing piece to this puzzle, she is the key, it is her spirit that has called this maze … so … I need to find the history of this house and who lived here" Derek explained, making his way to the lounge once more.

Standing at the entrance, Derek closed his eyes, taking a deep breath before looking at the piles of books that were before him, stacked neatly in piles long ways in several cupboards, before too long, his gaze became fixed on one pile in the far right corner of the room, a few, more dusty looking books, all bound in dark red binding leather.

Derek made his way over to the set of books, reaching for the central one, pulling it out to find it was a photo album.

Flicking through the various pages, he stopped at one in particular as Timothy came to stand beside him.

Staring up at Derek was a family photo of several people, Derek glazed his fingertips over the face of a young woman in the far right.

"This is her … this is the young woman whose spirit lives in the basement, Derek's breath hitched as he closed his eyes again, holding his hand above the photo slightly as Timothy looked at him in amazement.

"She was married … to this man here behind her … she was married off to him by her parents, she did not want to marry him … that is why she was put in the basement, she refused to start a family with him and she was silenced … it was frowned upon to go against your parents' wishes" Derek explained, placing the photo back under the mottled sheet of the photo album.

Suddenly a loud thud made the men turn their heads swiftly before Derek suddenly ran outside, Timothy struggling to keep up with him as one of his slippers fell off in the process.

"This is it … the maze is a symbol for her struggles, her life … the injustice … the maze is a symbol for her pain, the path she was forced to take … this maze is her journey … it's her heart!" explained Derek, as the men stood at the house entrance, looking at the labyrinth.

"I think … she wants me to help bring her to it … that's why it's here, the maze … in her houses … well … your house grounds, I can help her get through the labyrinth, the journey she took in life, but not reaching the light, she needs to get to the centre of it" Derek says, holding his hand up to the maze as Timothy stands behind him, astonished at the power this man held; the mazes vines began to move slightly, suddenly affected by the breeze as the sun hit its leaves like never before.

Suddenly, there was singing, Timothy turned to see nothing, no one, but still heard the sounds of a woman's voice carrying on the wind as it past him, moving closer to the maze as Derek began to walk into it slowly, the voice followed him.

"DEREK!" Timothy called, moving slightly towards the maze which moved towards him making him stop, unable to go any further.

Soon, the sound of the woman's voice couldn't be heard and Derek was out of sight, Timothy began to worry.

Soon, the mazes vines began to shrink in size, Timothy let out a deep breath in relief as he could see it was growing smaller in its height and width.

Then, up out of the remaining leaves and vines, Derek could be seen emerging from the centre of the maze which held a large stone statue, a statue of a young woman, with a smile on her face, her hand placed over her heart as the sun shun down on it.

"Sir … forgive me … I do not know what happened but …" Timothy turned to see Stephen, no longer the green cast statue he was a few days ago, now alive and well, soon to be followed by the voice of Muriel, her hat still intact, as if nothing had even occurred as she said.

"I am most upset, my tea has no doubt gone stone cold by now" she exclaimed as Timothy looked to Derek, as the men burst into laughter.

"All is well my good man" said Derek, as they all made their way into the house.

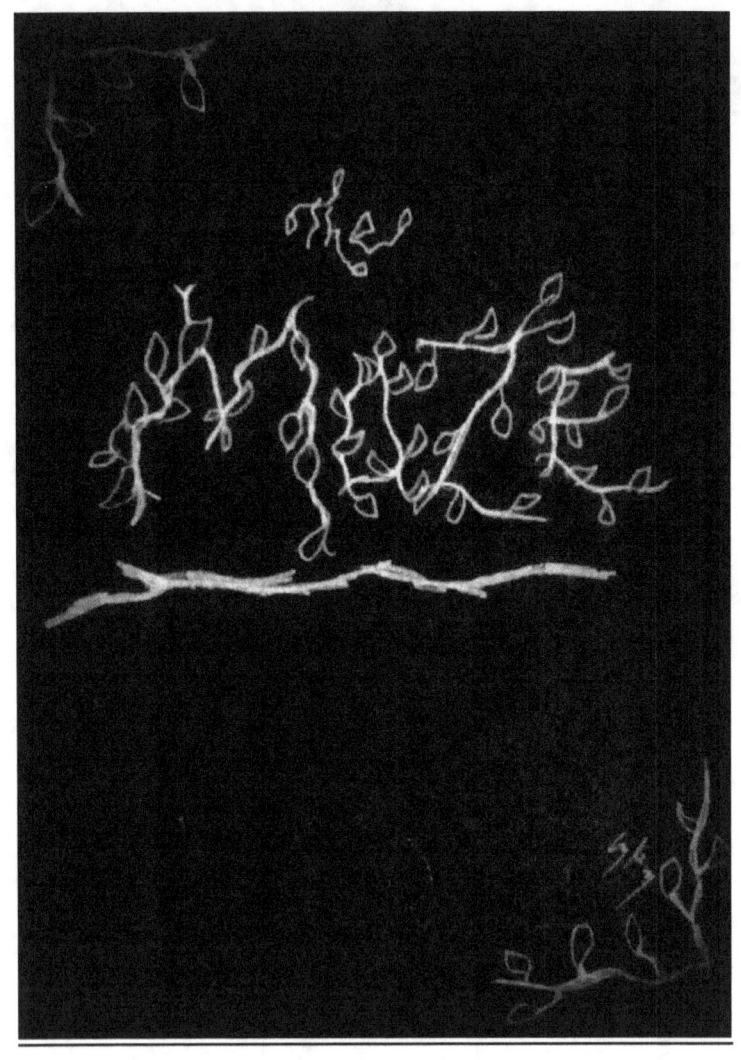

THE DRAGON EGG

Winter was always the hardest for our tame dragons, tamed by the keeper of their small town, a small town in medieval Europe. Dragons were frequent here and were used in war, as warriors and as war deterrents, to take down any enemy missiles.

One day, on a dark depressing morning in November, all the local folk were out in search of the festive parade where the dragons were displayed down the cobblestone street, locals in search also for festive gifts and food.

One young boy out with his Mother was distracted by a sparkling object that took his eye, slowly he walked away from his Mothers view to look at it more closely, to see it was a shell of a large oval egg, holding his small hands up to it he saw the depth of its size as his hands looked tiny next to it, he stared at its shimmering shell, covered in small scales in colours of blue, purple and green across its shell.

A small label upon it which said 'Dragon Egg' the boy looked at it with a glare of excitement in his eye as he asked the old hooded woman how much it was.

She told him,

"My dear boy, this is a very special dragons egg, for it has been held and examined by many dragon folk, it holds not one but two twin dragons in its luminous shell, this a very rare occurrence I've been told, twin dragons only come around once every hundred years, I'm afraid it will be too expensive for your pocket money my dear" she explained, patting the young boy on the head.

The boy frowned, the upset and annoyance plastered across his small freckled face, suddenly a family walked into the woman's sight as she greeted them, moving away from the young boy, noticing that she wasn't paying him any attention, he was suddenly filled with a feeling of mischievousness as he reached for the large egg with his small shaking hands, gripping it hard and wrapping it in the small blanket he was carrying, he grinned to himself, hiding a devilish chuckle as he began to make his way out of the shop unnoticed as the family took up most of the space, laughing and chattering away with the shop owner.

The young boy made it to the opposite side of the door, laughing he quickly re-joined his Mother who was not too far from sight.

"What is that you've got there boy … you haven't been snooping again have you … what have you done/" said the boy's Mother, grabbing the egg from the boys tight clutches and gasped.

"You naughty boy, you stole this? … Hey wait is this a …. A dragons egg?" she asked, her expression quickly changing from one of anger to one of intrigue as she looked down upon her Son.

"These are worth a lot of money my boy … we could eat for months if I sold this!" she exclaimed, hiding it under her large coat, patting her boy on the head as he frowned.

"But Mum I want it as a pet … the lady told me it was rare because it has twin dragons in it" said the boy, struggling to keep up with his Mother who was pacing quickly through the crowds of people.

"Twins … well then we can eat well for even longer … a pet … no my boy that won't do … dragons are very dangerous, not the sort of thing to be around my boy" she said simply, grabbing the boys hand and pulling him through the crowds.

"We will take it to Mr Baker … he will know what to do … he pays very well for rare things, well after a haggle from me and I fancy some of those festive pastries I've been smelling all day" she exclaimed with a smile.

Soon enough, they were brought to a very dark alleyway, the woman hesitated for a moment, turning to see her and her Son were the only two people there before taking hold of the door handle to the shop, a bell rung as they stepped in, making the boy jump in shock as he stayed close behind his Mother.

"Mr Baker … Hello … Mr Baker, I have something to show you" said the woman, her voice wavering off slightly as she her eyes landed on several unsavoury things in the man's shop, including taxidermy creatures and medieval torture items that made the woman's throat close.

Suddenly there was a noise in the distance, a rustling sound, followed by a loud thud which displayed Mr Baker jumping down from the loft hatch, his entrance looking as messy as his shop, the young boy jumped back, knocking into a large leather seat which squeaked, followed by a few rats running from underneath it to hide themselves under a small crack in the floor.

"Aww Amanda … how nice to see you again … what have you got for me? said Mr Baker, moving over to kiss her hand as she smiled slightly, moving over to the table for him to examine the product more closely.

The young boy, still close to his Mother looked at the man in thought, his eyes fixated on the large pile of items Mr Baker had just pulled from his grubby jacket pocket, the boy looked at them closely, seeing they were several eye glasses, in different sizes, as Mr Baker raised one to his eye, frowning to keep it in place over his eye like a monocle.

"Well … actually Tim, my boy here found it … he says it's a dragons egg … with twin dragons inside" said Amanda, gingerly handing it over to Tim who held out his hands eagerly.

Taking the egg in his hands, it looked to be quite heavy as his hands dipped slightly towards the table as he carried it over to grab a cloth and a matchbox.

"Well … little man … if you are right then … your Mummy is in for quite a bit of money but of course … I need to be sure it is in fact what you say it is Amanda .. You understand" Tim said with a sleazy smile, placing the egg carefully down on the cloth, he lit a match from the box and held it very close to the eggs surface.

Suddenly the egg moved, making Amanda step back and Tim laugh in amazement, the young boy smiled, placing his small hands over the edge of the counter to see the egg more closely.

"Well little man … you were right, it is a dragons egg … twins though … I will have to weigh this ... just a second" said Tim, carrying the egg over to the window and placing it slowly on the dusty set of metal scales, as soon as the egg touched the scales plate, the arrow pinged out of reading, breaking the glass monitor and springing across the shop floor.

"Well … I would say this is definitely twin dragons here … as my scales can't even weigh it … what was your name Son?" Tim asked, moving over to the floor to retrieve the arrow and placing it back on the counter.

"Percy Sir" said the boy, smiling over at his Mother who looked very pleased, knowing that this could mean a lot of money for her and her boy.

"Well Percy … if you come over here … to the till machine, you can help me count out the money for you and your Mum, what do you think?" Tim says as the yon nods and stands beside him as he opens the till.

"Hang on Tim … you haven't given me any indication of price … that's very unlike you … whenever I've brought things to you, we haggle price before you even step foot near the till … why is that?" she asks, moving over the window and picking up the dragons egg as Tim's eyes bulge slightly

"Oh no no … aha … don't misunderstand me Amanda … I'm just busy today and thought it best to put you out of your misery by getting straight to the point" explained Tim, who smiled half, taking a step towards her again as Percy stood looking up at both of them.

Amanda looked around the shop, turning her head and glancing out of the window for a moment.

"Busy … that's odd … we are your only customers … the alleyway is deserted too … the only time I have known of you getting straight to the price … is when you want to get rid of someone, which means that … this must be worth a lot more than you will be offering me … you know what … on second thought … my Son did say he would like to keep it and I don't like to be taken for a fool … good day Mr Baker … come on Percy" she said, reaching her hand out to signal Percy to follow her, as they made their way out of the shop, leaving Tim with his arm raised in the air in protest with a very confused look on his face.

Amanda and Percy sprinted back down the darkened alleyway, soon into the light of the parade which was still in full swing as Percy's eyes set upon the many lanterns which were filling the sky, the boy looking up, mesmerized by the small flames that made each lantern glow.

"Mummy … does this mean I can keep the dragons as pets?" Percy asked as they came to a stop, seeing his Mother take out a couple of coins from her pocket to buy a loaf of bread from the market stall.

"Yes Percy … but only because … I think we have something quite special here … look" she began, getting down to her knees to be eye level with her Son, taking hold of his arms softly.

"I want you to promise me something darling … do not let anyone have this egg, no matter what money they offer, for Mr Baker to go straight to his till without saying a word about its value must mean it has much more worth then we think, I want you to keep hold of it do you hear me?" she says softly, looking her boy in the eye as he nods simply with a smile.

Taking the bread in her hands she breaks some off and hands it to her boy who stuffs it quite messily into his mouth as his Mother takes off a few small pieces at a time for herself.

Suddenly there was a voice in the distance, getting louder by the second.

"Hey … that boys got a dragon egg … GET HIM!" said the voice of another child, pointing at Percy as others turned towards him, Amanda grabbed her Son quickly as they made their way through the crowds as they heard heavy footsteps follow them as they picked their feet up.

"Percy run … go to our hideaway ok, in case we get separated, I will meet you there, wait for me Percy … GO!" she screamed after him as he ran fast past everyone, leaving his Mother paces behind him as she came off at a nearby alley to catch her breath, seeing the crowd run after her Son, luckily, Percy's small size and slight body meant he was much faster than the crowds of people, so he soon became far in front of them; following the signs knowing where he had to go, a secret hideaway made up mainly of caves and trees.

Soon he was brought to a small cave next to some old oak trees, there he entered the dark cave and sat down, pulling up the blanket that his Mother had left there the last time they were here, he sat on the blanket, placing the egg in his lap and began to talk to it.

"I hope my Mummy will get here soon, she told me to wait, we come here quite a lot … to get away from things, we don't have a home anymore, we do stay with Daddy sometimes but he works away and doesn't think it's safe for us to stay there alone so we come here until he sends for us again … I get very lonely … My

Mummy does too, she works on the market stalls selling things we find to get money for food, I wish I could actually talk to you, maybe you would protect us" the boy croaks, putting his head down as a tear rolls down his cheek and lands on the egg shell, suddenly the egg moves and forms a small crack, the boy looks up startled and places the egg down on the floor in front of him.

Suddenly the egg begins to form cracks all over its shell, spreading across its purple, green and blue hues, Percy sat back slightly, beginning to worry as to just what might pop out of it, his Mother did originally warn that they would be too dangerous for a boy.

Then, he saw a wing spring out from the shell, a dark brown and red colour, soon to be followed by the other wing, the boy sat there amazed, seeing the creature trying to push its head through the top of the egg shell but failing he said,

"Oh … you poor thing, do you want me to help you?" he said, reaching for the egg,

"That would be great, thank you young Sir!" said a booming voice that made Percy jump, letting out a small scream,

"Oh I'm sorry Percy I didn't mean to startle you, my brother here is bigger than me so I can't break through the shell properly, there's just not enough room" says the voice.

"You … can talk … a dragon … that talks" stutters the boy, reaching for the egg again and peeling back the top of the egg to see a head appear.

"Strange I know … but yes, we can talk … if someone talks to us, many people are too scared to get near us and think us nothing but fighting creatures … they try to control us … so to emphasise our power we squawk and raw, but you my young Sir … actually talked to us, like a human, so we can show you the same curtesy" the dragon explained, punching away he rest of the shell with a flick of his strong tale. He was probably about 10 inches tall, laid next to him was his brother, looking to be asleep.

"You'll have to forgive him, he's very tired, he's my younger brother, not very bright but a heart of gold, well x3 hearts actually" said the dragon, moving its clawed feet onto the cold ground.

"Do you have a name?" asked Percy,

"No … I'll give you that honour young Sir … be sure to name my brother too, he should be waking up soon" replied the dragon, moving its wings slightly.

"O.K., I'll name you … Titan ... and your brother Moltan" said the boy, with a smile.

"Where's your Mother?" asked Titan, turning his head to see the cave empty apart from them, Moltan still fast asleep.

"She told me to come here and wait for her, we were being chased for the egg, I think they knew how expensive it would be to sell it so I ran straight here, she told me to keep going even if we got separated" said the boy, lowering his head again.

"I'm sure she will turn up soon enough young Sir … you must remember that your small legs are younger than hers, it may take her longer to get here" explained Titan, suddenly Moltan let out a very loud yarn, his mouth widening.

"Hey… morning mate, is it breakfast yet?" said Moltan, his voice not as deep or well-spoken as his brothers, it actually reminded Percy of the stall holders voices, friendly but not with charm, he actually detected a slight cockney accent.

Titan shook his head with a chuckle of his deep voice.

"No Moltan … we've just hatched and this is our owner Percy, he's just named us … so, I am Titan and you are Moltan" explained Titan, as Moltan made a move to stand up, only to fall over again, making Percy laugh.

"Moltan eh? … I like that ... Makes me sound … Brave and Ferocious AAARRRRGGGHHHH" he said trying to sound mighty, getting his legs to just about stand up straight.

Titan laughed again, turning to look at Percy who was stifling a giggle.

"You … Ferocious, you were clutching on to my wing as Mother gave birth to us you big goof!" said Titan, reaching his wing over to wrap around Moltan and hoist him over beside him.

"Cheers Bro …" Moltan said, as Titan shook his head again,

"As you can see Percy, we aren't exactly alike but he's my brother so I must look out for him" Titan said as Percy smiled and nodded.

"Hang on Titan, do I need to get you and Moltan some food, you do eat don't you?" Percy asked, as Titan tilted his head before snapping it round to look at Moltan who had just toppled over yet again to fall into a pile of rubbish, making Percy chuckle at his clumsiness.

"I'm sure the land around here is sufficient enough young Sir, there will be plenty of bugs around here for us do not fret" Titan says with absolute confidence.

"Oh but I must warn you, we do grow quite quickly, doubling our size by the day so don't be alarmed if by tomorrow evening we are nearing your height!" Titan says as Moltan nods his tiny head, emerging from the pile in the corner with a paper bag on his wing.

"Yeh Titans right, soon we will be bigger than you young squire" Moltan adds, finally finding his feet as he hobbles over to join the group.

Soon enough, the darkness covered the sky as night fell upon the cave, as if it wasn't dark and gloomy enough, luckily for Percy, he had two dragons as company.

The next morning, Percy awoke to an awful sound, as he quickly covered his ears to shield them from the shrill sounds that were coming from outside the cave, slowly, carefully, he stepped outside, to find Titan and Moltan screeching at each other, a sickening high pitched sound, quickly followed by laughter from the two dragons who turned to see the grimace on Percy's face to the loud sounds.

"Oh young Sir … Oh I hope we didn't disturb you … no worries, we were practising our fight cries, when a dragon is a day old from hatching, their throats are fully grown so … I thought we'd try out our voices" Titan explained as the young boy looked to see they had grown to double their size, they stood at Percy's waist now, just as Titan explained.

"Sorry if our screams are a bit shrill, they will deepen as the days follow, I know that seems amusing seeing as my speaking voice is very deep already" Titan chuckled as Percy began to dig up some soil to find the dragon brothers some bugs to eat.

"My Mother still hasn't shown has she?" asked Percy, his head lowered to the ground, his voice cracking as the upset in his voice surfaces.

"I'm sorry young Sir … I'm sure she is making it here as we speak" said Titan, walking over to Percy, stretching his wing out to him, resting it on Percy's shoulder.

"That's for sure!" said a voice, as Percy turned to see the face of his Mother, he shot up like a lightning bolt and ran to wrap his arms around his Mother, almost knocking her over as she smiled and kissed her boy on the head as she embraced him.

"What are … who …"she began, pointing over to the dragons who stood back slightly as they saw the fear in her eyes.

"Oh Mum, this is Titan and Moltan, they are my dragons, they hatched last night, they can talk" said Percy, his eyes beaming with excitement, taking his Mum's hand to lead her over to them.

"Nice to meet you Ma'am, I'm Titan, this is my brother Moltan, please don't be alarmed, we mean you and your Son no harm" said Titan who bowed his head slightly to Amanda who stood there in silence.

"Well … err … thank you for keeping my Son company dragons" she said, her voice just above a whisper as she bowed slightly to them as well, her legs shaking as she moved very gingerly as if awaiting an attack.

"Thank you Ma'am, your Son was talking to us last night whilst we were still in our shell, no human ever makes that move with us dragons, we are used as fighting creatures and mistreated as if we don't have feeling, your Son spoke to us, it's that kindness and non judgment that caused us to hatch and we talk as a result, we are now vowed to protect you and your family" explained Titan as Moltan stepped forward to join his brother, nodding in agreement.

Amanda stood in awe, as her fear slowly began to melt away as she turned to her Son and smiled.

"Thank you dragons, I mean … Titan, Moltan, we are quite poor really and have no solid home until Percy's Father gets back in town" she explained, pulling her Son close to her side as she hugged him.

"Aww I see, well Ma'am, we can see that times are hard for you … is this due to poor fortune or something more?" asked Titan, walking up to look Amanda in the eye as she averted her gaze in embarrassment, stroking her boys head and encouraging him to go and play with Moltan, safe guarding his ears from her and Titans conversation.

"Percy's Father works for a rather unsavoury group of individuals, hence why his home isn't safe when he is away, he lives in a very dangerous area, known for crime and violence, plus … all of our money was stolen from my families safe, he claims his group had nothing to do with it but I disagree, we are homeless because of him, which is why I get worried about Percy being around him" Amanda explained, turning to see her boy playing in the soil with Moltan.

"My dear, brave lady, you have no need to fear, we will protect you, we will develop powers over the coming days, powers that will enable you a home, riches and more, you need not surround yourself and Percy with any possible danger, we are here to serve Amanda, all will be well, I can promise you that" said Titan with a smile as tears filled her eyes, finally, her struggling would cease and her and her Son, would live safely and comfortably, with the help of their dragons.

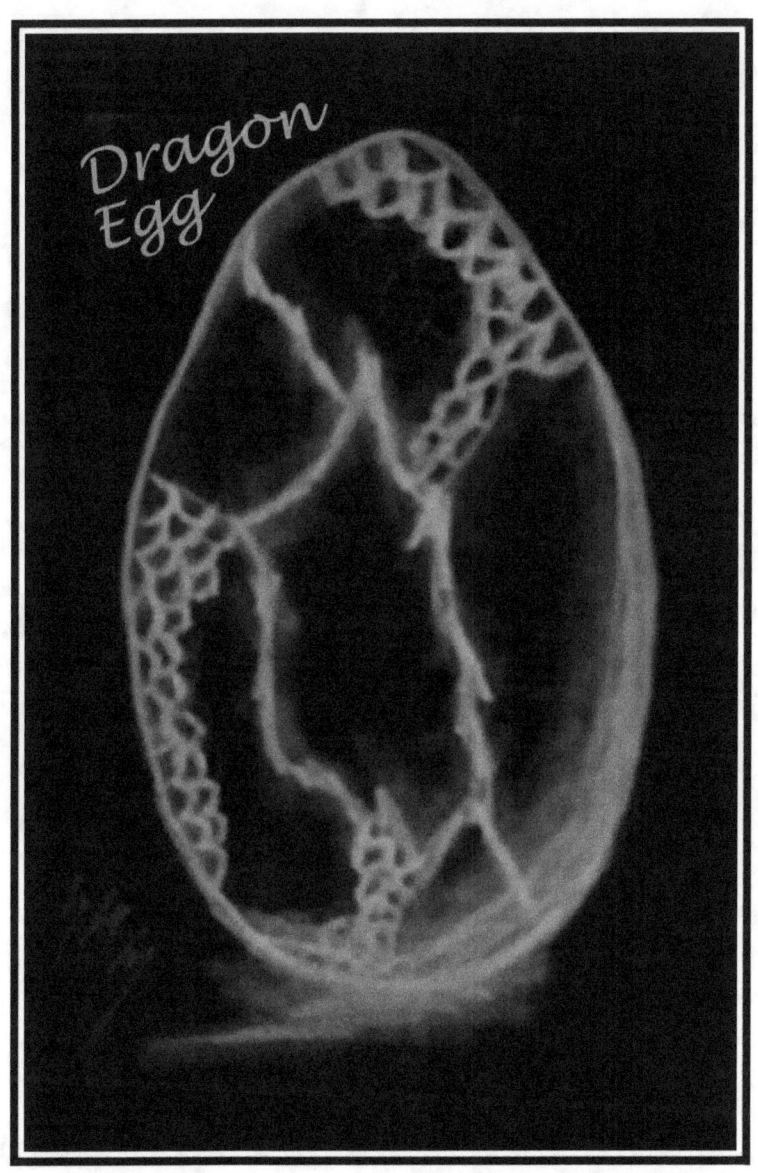

THE END

ABOUT THE AUTHOR

Emma Morrissey is a Fine Artist based in the U.K, a bachelor of the Arts with a Degree in the subject amongst her qualifications, since leaving University, she has become an entrepreneur by becoming a business woman.

Following several of her talents and skills, her interest and passion for Gothic culture has never wavered, taking inspiration from her own imagination, fashion, music, movies, theatre and literature. Aside from Emma's portraits, jewellery making and running workshops across Hampshire, the first time this passion came to light was in her first Gothic book 'Gothic Poetry – A collection from the crypt' filled with her own poems and illustrations.

Now comes the next part of her love for dark romance in this collection of dark short stories, if you would like to see more of Emma's work, you can buy her books from Amazon, search 'Emma Morrissey', or contact her via her website at:

Website - www.emzportraitscrafts.wordpress.com

Follow on Twitter - @emzportraits

Like on Facebook - www.facebook.com/emzportraitscrafts

119

"I hope you enjoy this latest instalment of my published works, I have truly been able to let my imagination run wild in the creation of these stories and have found it most enjoyable; keep your eyes on my website, for the latest news on my upcoming books and other events I will be attending, where you can purchase and order commissioned Artwork, buy a signed copy of my books and much more, thank you for purchasing this book, I hope you enjoy reading it as much as I have enjoyed writing it!" Emma Morrissey BA Hons 2016

www.ingramcontent.com/pod-product-compliance
Lightning Source LLC
Chambersburg PA
CBHW060428260626
47161CB00005B/1825